ALSO BY ROB WALKER

Significant Objects (coedited with Joshua Glenn)

Buying In

Letters from New Orleans

The Art of Noticing

The Art of Noticing

REDISCOVER WHAT REALLY MATTERS TO YOU

Rob Walker

Illustrations by Mendelsund/Munday

EBURY
PRESS

1 3 5 7 9 10 8 6 4 2

Ebury Press, an imprint of Ebury Publishing,
20 Vauxhall Bridge Road,
London SW1V 2SA

Ebury Press is part of the Penguin Random House group of companies
whose addresses can be found at global.penguinrandomhouse.com

Penguin
Random House
UK

First published in the United States by Alfred A. Knopf in 2019
First published in the United Kingdom by Ebury Press in 2019

www.penguin.co.uk

A CIP catalogue record for this book is available from the British Library

ISBN 9781529104431

DEDICATED TO E

CONTENTS

For anyone trying to discern what to do w/ their life:

PAY ATTENTION

TO WHAT

YOU PAY ATTENTION TO.

That's pretty much all the info u need.

AMY KROUSE ROSENTHAL

THE ART OF NOTICING: AN INTRODUCTION

'Pay attention', Susan Sontag once advised a young audience; she was speaking of the creative process, but also of living. 'It's all about paying attention. It's all about taking in as much of what's out there as you can, and not letting the excuses and the dreariness of some of the obligations you'll soon be incurring narrow your lives. Attention is vitality. It connects you with others. It makes you eager. Stay eager'.

To stay eager, to connect, to find interest in the everyday, to notice what everybody else overlooks – these are vital skills and noble goals. They speak to the difference between looking and seeing, between hearing and listening, between accepting what the world presents and noticing what matters to you.

This is important. It is also delightful. And it's the soul of this book.

THE ATTENTION OPPORTUNITY

Filmmaker James Benning once described an exercise from a class he taught called 'Looking and Listening' at the California Institute of the Arts. 'I'd take ten or twelve students someplace (an oil field in the Central

The one thing more than anything
else, is learning to pay attention.

ROBERT IRWIN

Valley, the homeless area near downtown Los Angeles, a kilometre-long hand-dug tunnel in the Mojave foothills, etc.), where they would head out on their own and practise paying attention', he later wrote.

The phrase *practise paying attention* really struck me when I read Benning's account in a book called *Draw It with Your Eyes Closed,* about creative assignments for art students. It stuck with me after.

I was at the time planning a five-week class I still teach once a year for the Products of Design graduate programme at New York's School of Visual Arts. Every year, at some point in our class, I ask my students to 'practise paying attention' before our next meeting. There are no other parameters. Each student resolves this deliberately vague request differently.

My ambition is to provoke them into thinking about what they notice, what they miss, why it matters, and how to become better, deeper and more original observers of the world and of themselves. And that, in turn, became the inspiration for this book.

Paying attention is a pretty vital skill for a designer. Then again, being what Saul Bellow called a 'first-class noticer' – cultivating the ability to attend to what others overlook, experiencing 'enchanting reality' as a new and fortuitous gift – is crucial to *any* creative process. And when I say 'creative process', I mean it as an idea that applies to a broad range of professions and pursuits. The scientist, the entrepreneur, the photographer, the coach: each relies on the ability to notice that which previously seemed invisible to everybody else.

Baseball executive Billy Beane found success by paying attention to data that others ignored.

Marine biologist Rachel Carson paid heroic attention to the scandalously obscured (and deadly) side effects of pesticides and thereby launched the modern environmental movement.

Warren Buffett paid attention to undervalued companies, becoming arguably the most successful investor of all time.

Jerry Seinfeld's 'observational' comedy brilliantly exploited a keen eye for the absurd lurking in what was taken for granted.

Artist and performer Laurie Anderson's remarkable eye for the hidden meanings in everyday language and culture made her an unlikely avant-garde superstar (and, as it happens, my all-time hero).

Anybody interested in thinking creatively seeks (needs) to notice what has been overlooked or ignored by others, to get beyond distractions and attend to the world. Every day, successful teachers, doctors, lawyers, small business owners and middle managers pick up on the subtle clues and details that sail past everyone else.

That, in fact, is why companies like Google and Goldman Sachs have introduced programmes specifically designed to help workers counteract our culture of distraction in order to regain their focus and creativity, often under the auspices of meditation or mindfulness training. It is why military leaders from Dwight Eisenhower to James Mattis have extolled the virtues of taking a determined break from interruption and intrusion to make informed and thoughtful decisions.

Paying attention, making a habit of noticing, helps cultivate an original perspective, a distinct point of view. That's part of what I try to teach my students, and it's part of what I try to practise myself.

But paying attention isn't easy.

THE ATTENTION PANIC

The stimulation of modern life, philosopher Georg Simmel complained in 1903, wears down the senses, leaving us dull, indifferent and unable to focus on what really matters.

In the 1950s, writer William Whyte lamented in *Life* magazine that 'billboards, neon signs,' and obnoxious advertising were converting the American landscape into one long roadside distraction.

'A wealth of information creates a poverty of attention', economist Herb Simon warned in 1971.

The sense that external forces seek to seize our attention isn't new – but it feels particularly acute today. Billboards, shop windows, addictive digital games, an endless news cycle and commercial appeals tantalise us from all directions. We contend with the myriad distractions flowing through the pocket-size screens we carry with us everywhere. By various estimates, a typical smartphone owner checks a device 150 times per day – every six minutes – and touches, swipes, or taps it more than 2,500 times.

It can feel like everyone we've ever known, every business or cause, wants – demands – to claim our attention. *Polyconsciousness* is what one researcher termed the resulting state of mind that divides attention between the physical world and the one our devices connect us to, undermining here-and-now interactions with actual people and things around us.

Perhaps we have reached peak distraction. Certainly a raft of eloquent critics have articulated what amounts to a twenty-first-century attention panic. In fact, many have complained about the influence of devices *by means of their devices*. #FOMO amounts to an endlessly trending topic about our unhealthy obsession with . . . trending topics.

But you know all that. And this book is not here to add to the attention

Over the coming century, the most vital

human resource in need of conservation

and protection is likely to be our own

consciousness and mental space.

TIM WU

panic. To the contrary, it is here to offer you a helpful suggestion: if we've reached peak distraction, then taking the time to pause and pay attention has never been so important.

And the good news is that we have the ability to do this.

It's true, as many have observed, that human distractibility – the way we're instinctively drawn to the proverbial bright and shiny objects – is hardwired, a function of evolution.

But it's also true that, more than any other creature, humans can outmanoeuvre our own base instincts. That's why it's no coincidence that peak distraction has coincided for instance with a vogue for meditation and mindfulness: We *know* we're distracted and we yearn to see the world more clearly. We also know we can learn to direct our attention where we wish to.

What we do with our attention, in short, is at the heart of what makes us human.

THE JOY OF NOTICING

Deep attention is good for the soul.
But unfortunately, it doesn't always *feel as* important as it is. With growing demands and endless to-do lists, we can be understandably reluctant to try something new, to experiment and to let curiosity take us out of the usual.

We want, instead, to feel busy.

But being busy is overrated. Darwin worked only a couple of hours a day and spent a lot of time taking long walks. No matter what line of work you're in or what kind of life you lead, you will know how easy it is to spend a day getting stuff done . . . without doing anything meaningful at all. A hypereffective schedule designed to maximise productivity is, in fact, more likely to distract you from what's important than help you discover it.

Imagine, instead, devoting just one hour a *week* to consciously directing your attention. How would that affect the way you see, perceive and think? How would it shift the way you engage with the world? How much might that not only change but also improve your work and your life?

How *fun* would that be?

That is exactly what this book will help you find out. It is comprised of exercises and provocations meant to help you counter distraction by inspiring you to make the small yet enjoyable effort to rediscover your sense of creativity and wonder. These ideas are meant to shake up the way you see, hear, notice and otherwise experience the world.

They came from my students, conversations with clever and generous friends, thoughtful strangers, my own habits, behavioural psychologists, artists, writers, creators, entrepreneurs and all kinds of other people.

When you actively notice new things, that puts you

in the present . . . As you're noticing new things,

it's engaging, and it turns out . . . it's literally,

not just figuratively, enlivening.

ELLEN J. LANGER

Maybe one of these exercises could prompt you to write a ground-breaking novel or create a hit Instagram account or find an unlikely business opportunity. In fact, I hope that happens for you!

But this book treats the art of noticing as something more profound than a step in a creative process. It's an escape from the cult of productivity and efficiency – those impulses that shaped the causes of our attention panic in the first place.

Let's stop trying to be so productive all the time and make an effort to be more curious. Do you want to look back on a life of items crossed off lists drawn up in response to the demands of others? Or do you want to hang on to and repeat and remember the thrill of discovering things on your own?

Todd B. Kashdan, a professor of psychology at George Mason University, refers to curiosity as **'joyous exploration'** – defined as 'the recognition and desire to seek out new knowledge and information, and the subsequent joy of learning and growing'.

This book means to serve that spirit of curiosity and joy, whether it's in the service of productive aims or leisure.

You can use it in several ways.

HOW TO USE THIS BOOK

You can read *The Art of Noticing* straight through or you can skip around and graze where you wish, whenever you feel the need or urge to.

Pick and choose the aspects of noticing you wish to explore or enjoy. Treat it like a learning experience; treat it like a game. The choice, by design, is yours.

The 131 exercises that follow are 131 opportunities for joyous exploration in all its dimensions. You can act on them or treat them as thought experiments. Either way, they are 131 opportunities for you to do or think about something new and different.

Sometimes that means letting the mind wander; sometimes that means making sure it doesn't.

Sometimes it's about finding a pocket of stillness and sometimes it's about wilful activity in the most unlikely circumstances.

Sometimes it means blocking all distraction and sometimes it means choosing the distractions you want the most. It's about being in a moment or escaping one.

Every day is filled with opportunities to be amazed, surprised, enthralled – to experience the enchanting everyday. To stay eager. To be, in a word, alive.

The Art of Noticing

Each of the exercises and suggestions that follow is ranked by degree of difficulty, from 1 to 4:

SO EASY Anybody can do this, right now.

DOABLE This may take some planning or forethought, but it's nothing you can't handle.

ENJOYABLY CHALLENGING You'll make an effort – but it will be worth it.

ADVANCED Noticing has become an adventure.

1

LOOKING

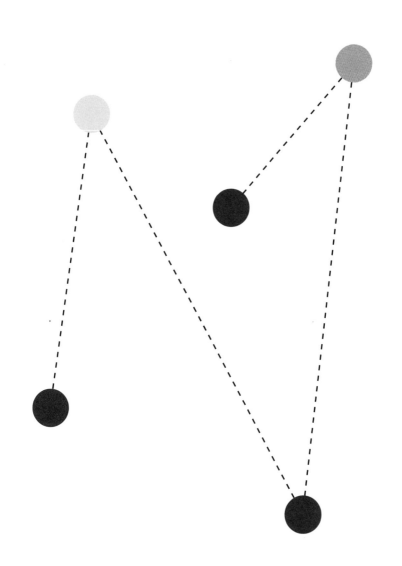

CONDUCT A SCAVENGER HUNT

👁 👁

A few years ago, I was in San Francisco, a city I'd visited at least a half-dozen times before. With no spare moments for sightseeing, I decided to look, wherever I went, for security cameras.

This exercise lacked an obvious point. I'm interested in the proliferation of surveillance technology, but on this trip, I was not conducting research. I just wanted to inject some novelty into the way I saw neighbourhoods I'd seen before. It was a game – a single-object scavenger hunt, played for the fun of noticing.

I didn't know it at the time, but I was creating a mental *search image*. That's a term I'm borrowing from the writer and psychology professor Alexandra Horowitz, who in turn credits it to a noted bird watcher, Luuk Tinbergen. Tinbergen noticed that songbirds tend to seek out a specific species of beetle (or whatever) that they evidently prefer to devour over other edible insects. Having a predetermined search image helps them spot their prey of choice.

Creating a mental search image, Horowitz explains, is how 'we find our car keys, spot our friends in a crowd and even find patterns that we had never seen before'. In her useful and fun book *On Looking,* she writes: 'Everyone needs a mechanism to select what, out of all the things in the world, they should both look for and at, and what they should ignore'. That's a search image – 'the visual form of the expectation that allows you to find meaning in chaos'.

In San Francisco, security cameras turned out to be more pervasive than I would have guessed. Some were stealthily placed, while others were aggressively visible, presumably as deterrents to would-be criminals. To this day, I now notice cameras wherever I go.

This was my first experience in a practise of conscious noticing that has blossomed into an obsession. I find objects and recurring features in a variety of environments. The trick is to choose something that's ubiquitous and taken for granted. I've studied pay phones (where are they clustered, where are they rare, how many are broken?) and standpipes (which ones have been modified to prevent their use as de facto stools?) and neighbourhood watch signs (which neighbourhoods have them and which don't?). I've looked in big cities and small communities, at home and on the road.

At times there was a tangible payoff: I wrote about the defacement of neighbourhood watch signs in Savannah, Georgia (which rather undercut the message of vigilant safety) and about standpipes adorned with spiky add-ons whose only function is to keep anyone from resting on them.

But mostly my scavenger hunts are just entertaining – and addictive. In San Francisco, I took pictures of some of the security cameras I spotted. When I called my wife from the airport at the end of that trip, I marvelled to her about the astonishing array of surveillance technology I noticed. 'Please', she said, '*do not* wander around an airport photographing the security cameras'. Good point. Sometimes it's better just to look – or rather, to see.

Paying attention

is the only thing that guarantees insight.

It is the only real weapon we have against power, too.

You can't fight things you can't actually see.

MICHELLE DEAN

SPOT SOMETHING NEW EVERY DAY

A heightened observational mind-set takes over when we're tourists. In a new place, we pay attention to *everything,* it seems. (Ecologist Liam Heneghan has given this 'heightened and delighted attention to the ordinary', which manifests in someone new to a place, a name: *allokataplixis*, combining the Greek *allo*, meaning 'other', and *katapliktiko*, meaning 'wonder').

But we spend most of our time in familiar places that have lost their inherent novelty. We take these surroundings for granted and we stop paying close attention. A recurring commute becomes profoundly numbing. Psychologists who study perception call this phenomenon *inattentional blindness.*

One of my students pledged to 'notice something new' every day on the five minute walk she made to and from our classroom studios. You can do the same from a bike, car, bus or train. No tech tools are required.

Watch for:

SECURITY CAMERAS

ABANDONED PAY PHONES

NEIGHBOURHOOD WATCH SIGNS

**ANYTHING NATURAL (A PLANT, A ROGUE BIRD)
IN AIRPORTS**

LOCKSMITH STICKERS

WEEDS

EMPLOYEE OF THE MONTH PLAQUES

STRAY SHOPPING TROLLEYS

STRAY TRAFFIC CONES

ABANDONED BIKE LOCKS

HAND-PAINTED SIGNS

MOBILE PHONE TOWERS

TAKE A COLOUR WALK

As part of a class about colour, artist Munro Galloway assigned students a one-hour walk. 'Let colour be your guide', he instructed. 'Allow yourself to be sensitized to the colour in your surroundings'.

Think about these questions from Galloway's description of the exercise in *Draw It with Your Eyes Closed:*

- What are the colours that you become aware of first?

- What are the colours that reveal themselves more slowly?

- What colours do you observe that you did not expect?

- What colour relationships do you notice?

- Do colours appear to change over time?

START A COLLECTION

👁 👁

In 1977, furniture designer George Nelson published a book boldly titled *How to See,* an expansion of an earlier pamphlet written for the Department of Health, Education and Welfare. Twenty-five years later, Design Within Reach founder Rob Forbes oversaw an improved republication of the volume. It's mostly a collection of pictures taken by Nelson, who observed that the work might have more honestly been titled *How I See.* In a new introduction Forbes called it 'a book about the discipline of recording and assessing visual information'.

Nelson was a collector and he excelled at dreaming up interesting search images to hunt and document: arrows, public clocks, manhole covers, street corners, geometric shapes, specific architectural details, signs and objects prohibiting specific behaviours, ephemeral traces such as footprints – human, animal or even (if you include tyre treads) mechanical.

Nelson's hunts were sometimes more conceptual. For instance, he searched for *contrast*. He wrote: 'Look for hardness and softness and the contrast between these two qualities'. *How to See* included images of a flag outside a building, contrasting the rippling cloth and the solid wall; of the contrast between soft lips and hard teeth; and of a blimp – a pliable thing 'rigidified' by air. 'Isolating the qualities of hard and soft gets us to look in a special way', Nelson observed.

About a dozen years after bringing Nelson's book back into the world, Forbes published his own set of photo collections under the title *See for Yourself.* His searches included house numbers in Charleston and sewer tiles in San Francisco, along with more abstract angles and curves, texture and repetition, as well as contrasts between the very new and very old, the natural and the built, the colourful and the drab, the crumbling and the pristine. My favourite of Forbes's image series documents the surprising visual and physical diversity of bike locks in Amsterdam – 'studies in materials and textures and colours as much as function', he writes.

'It's about observation and thinking', Forbes argues. 'When you discover something special out there it's like stumbling into a café or shop that was not listed in a tourist guide – your experience of the world is much richer because you did it on your own'.

COUNT WITH THE NUMBERS YOU FIND

George Nelson's best image collection may have been a set of numbers that he turned into a slide show. 'Finding numbers in the urban landscape is very easy, and looking for them is a good eye-sharpening exercise', he wrote. His slide show started with a picture of the number 100 and counted down to 0. (It took him months to collect all the images.)

While travelling by foot, bike or car, start 'counting' and see how far you can get.

'The hunt was more satisfying and the reward was a new awareness of something previously invisible', Nelson observed. 'The game, of course, is to find unexpected shapes, sizes and contexts'.

Look for a 1, then a 2, then a 3 and keep going; stop at the end of your current journey or carry it over to the next one and the next one, for a week, a month, a year . . . or the rest of your life.

DOCUMENT THE (SEEMINGLY) IDENTICAL

👁 👁

A developer named Jacob Harris regularly takes pictures of a blue cloudless sky – near-identical squares of blue. He calls the series 'Sky Gradients'.

The tight constraints of the project are the point; Harris cites the influence of Dogme 95, a filmmaking movement from the 1990s started by Danish directors Lars von Trier and Thomas Vinterberg. They created a manifesto that advocated the power of story but was notable for its emphasis on restrictions – against lighting and filter tricks or other special effects, among other limitations.

Harris suggests that his real motive has little to do with sparking creativity. 'I don't really consider myself much of an artist or this project as art', he wrote in TheAtlantic.com. 'I do this as a means of meditation'. While sometimes inspired by a fleeting moment of boredom, Harris claims he takes these pictures 'not to kill time but to memorialise it, albeit in a pointedly abstract way'.

Sometimes, he says, he forgets where he took a photograph or precisely why. 'Much like writing it down in a journal or throwing a stone into the water, to mark the moment is also to let it pass', he observes. 'I often don't have a pen, and I'm usually not near rocks or ponds. But I always have my phone. And sometimes even when I am sad, it's still a beautiful sunny day. I reach into my pocket for my phone and point it towards the sky. I exhale and take a photo'.

My friend (but not relation) Dave Walker has a similar pastime. He takes pictures of telephone poles around New Orleans. Close-ups – details, really. Sometimes the image shows the texture of a pole, but sometimes a pole is riddled with staples or touched by an odd dab of paint or marred by a bent nail. The colours vary and subtle patterns appear. I think of Dave when I notice a telephone pole as I'm walking and study it for some quietly hidden visual appeal that he might spot.

Pavements, car parks, grass, tree trunks – both human-made features and natural ones offer endless possibilities.

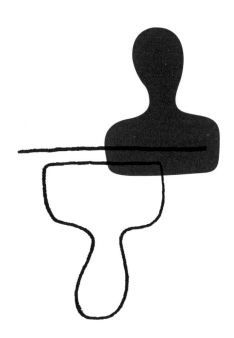

LOOK SLOWLY

The artist Robert Irwin is surely the patron saint of noticing. As detailed in Lawrence Weschler's book *Seeing Is Forgetting the Name of the Thing One Sees,* Irwin's work focuses on the experience and context of seeing, rather than on producing art objects – 'allowing people to perceive their perceptions', as Weschler put it.

Irwin started out as a painter but spent lots of time staring at his canvas, not painting anything at all. He obsessed over the details of the gallery spaces where his work was displayed – the angles, the floorboards, the light. He once spent eight months in Spain, producing nothing.

'I found a certain strength in sustaining over a period of time my attention on a single point', Irwin told Weschler. 'After a while, it's like you peel back the layers of that issue and are able to get to a much deeper reasoning of how and in what way this thing makes sense'. Gradually he transitioned to making work such as acrylic discs that treated light as their medium. He made 'site-dependent' work, installations that transformed the way we see a particular space.

It's possible to borrow Irwin's practise and apply it on a more practical scale. Slow Art Day offers an example. This is an annual event held at multiple locations across the United States; participants are invited to meet at a museum, SlowArtDay.com explains, and 'look at five works of art for 10 minutes each, and then meet together over lunch to talk about their experience'.

You don't have to wait for the next Slow Art Day to try this. It's fun to spend such time with a work of art, but you can also look at five products at your local department store for ten minutes each.

Simple as this sounds, it's quietly radical. A study by the Metropolitan Museum of Art in New York concluded that its patrons spend a median seventeen *seconds* in front of any given painting. Start with Slow Art Day's ten-minute benchmark. You'll get a glimpse of what drives Irwin's remarkable process: You'll see details you missed, you'll draw new connections and you'll reconsider first impressions.

We spend so much time looking down at our phones or our feet, or even just from side to side into store windows, that it's a good idea to remind ourselves to look up towards the tops of buildings. This is where cornucopiate garlands and angry gryphons gather below eaves and the residue of old advertising signage lingers.

ALICE TWEMLOW

LOOK UP – AND THEN LOOK FURTHER UP

Every year, at least one of my students hits on some variation of the idea that if you want to notice things you missed in the past, then *up* is a good place to explore. For starters, you can simply look up from your phone from time to time. Lift your eyes to what's not right in front of you, but just above.

The design writer Alice Twemlow, whom I got to know after she founded what became the School of Visual Arts' Design Research graduate programme, points out that there's a good reason so many people who think about attention suggest that taking a moment to look up can be powerful: 'Because it's true'.

That's a great start. But Twemlow has another thought: looking *further* up.

'If you look further up – and you really have to crank your head back for this, which means slowing way down or stopping moving altogether – to the roofs themselves', she says, 'you might glimpse drying washing being whipped by the wind, a flock of pigeons homing, prisoners playing basketball in a fenced-in yard, or someone secretly sunbathing in between the jagged teeth of water towers, chimneys and aerials'.

Up is a place that might be glimpsed while in motion.

Further up requires the suspension of movement and activity.

'My favourite is to count chimneys', suggests designer and writer Ingrid Fetell Lee. 'Looking for chimneys raises your gaze, which seems to boost your mood (possibly because it lets more light into the eye), but it also makes you look at a completely different part of a city or a town. You become aware of the way the land meets the sky, the various ways that roofs are built, and the wildlife living up in the rafters and the treetops'.

Editor and writer Sarah Rich once said to me: 'I'd say one visual experience I have more now is seeing planes and birds WAY high in the sky, which requires looking up for a while. It's sort of like daytime satellite spotting'. The further up you look, the more time it takes to see anything.

Find a place to sit or lie down and look up. Take your time. See what's up there. Then look for what's beyond that.

REPEAT YOUR POINT OF VIEW

One student of mine, Steve Hamilton, noticed an 'incongruous bench' not far from our classroom that, he realised, 'no one sits on'. He made a habit of occupying this spot for fifteen minutes every day and studying passersby.

Lots of perfectly familiar settings would suit. Sit by an office window that you hardly bother to glance through anymore or on your own front step. The determined repetition of the same view over time will likely reveal something that is not really the 'same view' after all.

LOOK OUT A WINDOW

Spend ten minutes looking out the window you most persistently ignore. Find one in your office or your bedroom or wherever, the one you so take for granted that you forget it's even there.

Examine the edges of what the window makes visible. Find three things you've never noticed. Describe the scene in front of you.

Next time you encounter a window that's new to you, stop and look. Study the view. Tally the details. Look for movement. Think about what you can't control. See what happens.

Windows are a powerful existential tool . . . The only thing you can do is look. You have no influence over what you will see. Your brain is forced to make drama out of whatever happens to appear. Boring things become strange.

SAM ANDERSON

REFRAME THE FAMILIAR

Another student of mine, Lucy Knops, was inspired by Robert Irwin's habit of seeing. She thought about how she *framed* what she saw. She made physical Polaroid-size frames, acrylic with a dry-erase surface – like portable windows. 'Hold the frame up to an object or scene and write a one- to two-word description on it', she instructed. Maybe that's a word like *beautiful* or *vacant* or *cloudy*.

'Then', she continued, 'shift the frame to focus on a different subject, leaving the original description'. How does the earlier description influence what you're looking at?

The idea echoes one from Sister Corita Kent, a nun and artist who in her book *Learning by Heart: Teachings to Free the Creative Spirit* proposed using 'an instant finder', which was an empty 35mm slide holder – a viewfinder with no camera. You can make your own by cutting a rectangular hole in a chunk of cardboard and using it to narrow and reframe your vision: 'It helps us to take things out of context', Kent and her coauthor, Jan Steward, wrote. '[It] allows us to see for the sake of seeing'.

LOOK REALLY, *REALLY* SLOWLY

👁 👁 👁

In her art history classes, Jennifer L. Roberts makes her students regard a single work for 'a painfully long time'. How long, exactly? Three hours. Her students, not surprisingly, resist the idea.

'It is commonly assumed that vision is immediate', Roberts has written. "It seems direct, uncomplicated and instantaneous – which is why it has arguably become the master sense for the delivery of information in the contemporary technological world. But what students learn in a visceral way in this assignment is that in any work of art there are details and orders and relationships that take time to perceive'.

When their resistance dies down, Roberts reports, her students find that looking really, *really* slowly forces them to notice things they had initially passed over, sometimes changing their entire understanding of a work. The process unlocks meaning and potential that first glances can miss.

This can be applied well beyond the context of contemplating works of art. Look really, really slowly at almost anything and chances are good you'll see more than you ever could have imagined.

LOOK REPEATEDLY

In an essay in *The New York Times,* culture reporter Randy Kennedy described a decade or so of going to look again and again at Caravaggio's *The Denial of St Peter* at the Metropolitan Museum of Art. Over the years, his view of the work evolved. He used to think Peter was its primary focus but has come to to regard another figure, the maid who has called him out (per the Gospels) as a follower of Jesus, as the work's truly central subject. He now believes it is her 'hesitation and humanity' in a moment of accusation that gives the painting its power.

Kennedy shrugs off the possibility that this take, developed over so many years, might contradict historical evidence or more official art-critic interpretations. 'One result of looking at a painting so long that you can see it in your mind's eye is that it does, in a very real sense, become your own', he writes, 'not quite the same painting that anyone else will see'.

This could be replicated with almost any image or object. Devote time to studying something you've seen before. You can look over and over – until, like Kennedy, you are seeing something in a way that nobody else could.

What to Look for
When You're in a Museum

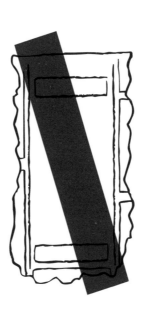

PLAY BUY, BURN OR STEAL

Many people, Nick Gray points out, just aren't comfortable in museums. So his company, Museum Hack, offers tours specifically designed to combat that unease, partly by demystifying hushed and revered spaces. 'The strategy', he says, 'is to get people to fall in love with museums, to get more people to go to more museums more often'.

Partly this means getting highly informed and energetic guides giving frankly opinionated tours. Partly it means cluing participants into basics such as what an accession number means or how to do their own research. Sometimes it means getting museum-goers to approach a collection in a manner different from whatever the curators had in mind – like seeking out the piece with the highest acquisition cost. And it almost always means using on-the-fly games and challenges to prod participants into interacting with the art and one another in an honest and unpretentious way.

One clever example involves the game Buy, Burn or Steal. Participants are challenged to examine all the works in a particular gallery and decide which one they'd be willing to buy, which one they so despise that they'd like to burn it and which one they love so much that they want to steal it.

The best thing about Buy, Burn or Steal is that you can play it anywhere, alone or with others.

STUDY EVERYTHING EXCEPT THE ART

A museum is a space carefully designed to direct your attention. You are meant to look at what is on display – the art, the historical artifacts, the scientific specimens, whatever – and any related wall text or supporting information. The lighting, the layout and everything else encourage you to notice precisely what the curators have set before you, nothing more.

I wonder sometimes if the structured formality of the museum-going experience leads to the curiously sheep-like or even disengaged behaviour that's routine among certain patrons. If you've ever been to a museum that houses a particularly iconic work – Leonardo da Vinci's *Mona Lisa* at the Louvre, Rembrandt's *The Night Watch* in Amsterdam's Rijksmuseum – you know exactly what I mean: everyone is so busy snapping pictures of these works by means of their phone or other device that nobody seems to be *looking* at them at all. (And meanwhile, of course, the building is filled with other significant but less famous works that could be contemplated at length without a mosh pit.) Some museum-goers take this one step further by focusing mostly on snapping selfies and documenting their proximity to great works they're not even paying attention to.

If treating the museum as a backdrop has become almost a parody – see me (sort of) seeing what I'm supposed to see? – then maybe the more productive strategy is to pay attention to something else. *Anything* else.

Next time you're at a museum of any kind then, devote some time to studying what is not on display. Here is your checklist:

LOOK FOR FLAWS

'You usually come to a museum and orient yourself towards the artworks', artist Nina Katchadourian has observed, 'and a lot of things in your literal and metaphorical peripheral vision are ruled out as things not worth looking at'. But questioning what deserves attention and what doesn't helped guide Katchadourian to an unusual project she called 'Dust Gathering', an audio tour of the Museum of Modern Art centred entirely on the museum's dust: where it collects, who cleans it, how it's kept to a minimum and so on. To create this tour, she interviewed behind-the-scenes personnel extensively – but she also got used to the idea of zeroing in on the existence of dust bunnies in the crisply pristine museum.

'It's weird to go there and feel a domestic sense of that building now', Katchadourian later told an interviewer. 'It's brought it down to earth in a strange way for me. I always found MoMA intimidating and kind of a temple'. And of course that is part of what museums are designed to make visitors feel: the sense of reverence is a big part of the power to direct your attention. Challenge that.

CONSIDER THE GUARDS

What they're wearing, their expressions, what they're looking at. Imagine their relationship to the work on display. Don't make assumptions and don't bother them. (You'd be surprised how many journalistic and photographic projects have focused on museum guards.) Just think about them.

PAY ATTENTION TO THE NAMES OF DONORS

In almost any museum, you will encounter various wall-panel displays thanking specific donors and patrons, as well as the names given to individual galleries and halls within the museum. Research these people.

STUDY THE BEHAVIOUR OF OTHER MUSEUM-GOERS

Photographer Stefan Drashan is an inspiration on this front. He spends quite a bit of time in museums, observing and documenting other people and, somewhat secondarily, their relationship to displayed works. One series is called 'People Touching Artworks', an activity that is almost always verboten but turns out to be fairly commonplace just the same. Another series collects images of people sleeping in museums. Yet another, 'People Matching Artworks', captures patrons in outfits that pair eerily well with the paintings they're looking at or walking past. Start by stealing these categories. Then invent your own.

LISTEN TO WHAT OTHER PATRONS SAY TO ONE ANOTHER OR WHAT THE STAFF SAY TO THEM

Musician/artist John Kannenberg once created 'A Sound Map of the Art Institute of Chicago', recording various casual snippets. 'No flashes', a guard warned patrons near *American Gothic*, for instance. In another gallery, he captured an exchange he summarises as 'visitor questions the quality of the Art Institute's Impressionism collection while speaking with security'. Follow his example and listen to what's going on around you.

CONDUCT AN UNRELATED ACTIVITY

Maybe it's worth playfully accepting the notion of a museum as mere background, an environment we inhabit incidentally, as we do other things. What can those other things be? Several museums have experimented with opening their spaces to early-morning or off-hour meditation or yoga sessions. Come up with your own physical and mental health regimen suitable to your favourite museum. Share it with others.

TUNE INTO OBJECTS THAT COULD BE ART

In a somewhat infamous incident in 2016, a prankster left a pair of glasses on the floor of a San Francisco Museum of Modern Art gallery – where it was soon surrounded by (picture-taking) patrons believing the spectacles to be an artwork. This kind of thing has happened repeatedly. Why? Museums are a specialised context, the writer Tom Vanderbilt has pointed out, and 'have been called a "way of seeing", perhaps even a training ground for looking at the wider world'. This, he suggests, helps explain why a fixture or fire extinguisher can be mistaken for art. In short, we're primed to see art in museums, so everything looks like art.

Perceive these places for what they are and you'll perceive what's in them even more clearly.

MAKE IT ART

My wife and I were once wandering through a contemporary art museum when we entered a small gallery that contained nothing but two huge wooden crates. I puzzled over them because I wasn't sure if these crates were full of art waiting to be unpacked or if they themselves were art.

Idiotically, I searched for clues – either a little placard on the wall with the relevant name and provenance data (it's art!) or some kind of practical shipping sticker on the crates themselves (it *contains* art!). Unable to find conclusive evidence either way, we talked it over and decided to resolve the matter by way of our own declaration: the crates were art.

This was a silly attempt to make each other laugh, but it made us think of Marcel Duchamp and the urinal he signed and submitted to the Society of Independent Artists. The piece might have been his most famous and lasting provocation. Duchamp repurposed existing words and images and with a simple gesture redrew a boundary between the everyday and the elevated: art is what I say it is.

Think then of some regular walk or drive or ride you experience often or even that you're experiencing for the first time. Imagine yourself a curator. Decide what, among the things you notice, you might declare to be public works of art.

Perhaps a dishevelled pylon marking a street flaw that ought to have been fixed by now. Maybe a post that seems to be a lingering remnant of an otherwise departed fence. Possibly even a child with a piercing stare.

Grant yourself the superpower of making 'art' wherever you go, and see how that changes what you perceive.

Art is everywhere, if you say so.

DISCOVER THE BIG WITHIN THE SMALL

Alex Kalman is the curator of an unusual museum – called Mmuseumm –
on the little-trafficked one-block Cortlandt Alley in lower Manhattan. The
exhibition space is 1.8 metres square and used to be part of a freight lift
shaft. The objects on view are just as distinct as the room they occupy;
Kalman calls them examples of the 'vernacular', but they might look, to
some, like random items. In fact, they reflect a remarkable eye for the
deeper meaning that can lurk in the overlooked.

'These objects weren't created to be appreciated as pieces of art', Kalman said on one of my visits. And yet they reveal 'our psychology, our
needs, and our desires', he insisted. 'Some element of who we are'.

Kalman fits a remarkable and rotating variety of items on the slender shelves that line Mmuseumm's tight walls. He pointed out a small
sign, maybe 5 cm square, evidently from a motel. 'Dear Guest', it read,
because of the 'popularity of our guest room amenities', various items in
the room are for sale: $25 for the alarm clock, $15 for a hand towel, and
so on. 'Should you decide to take these articles from your room instead
of obtaining them from the Executive Housekeeper, we will assume you
approve a corresponding charge to your account'.

Translated: steal what you want and we will charge you for it. 'This
object', explains Mmuseumm's catalogue, 'is the result of a capitalist's
handling of crime'.

This sweeping sentiment can be pinned on an insignificant item
because of Kalman's remarkable ability to look and see. He openly
acknowledges the influence here of his parents, designer Tibor Kalman
and artist Maira Kalman. 'Every household has a first language, a kind

of language of the home', he says. 'And luckily for me the language of my home was looking; I was just kind of raised to look around'.

This means Kalman was also raised to discover the surprising within the workaday, by way of seeing deeply. He remembers, for instance, coming home from school one day to find someone installing a collection of onion rings – the kind you'd get from a greasy spoon – with 'unbelievable precision', in the living room. His parents, evidently, had decided these objects were worth serious consideration. In short, Kalman has spent 'a lifetime of looking carefully', he said, 'and seeking out the humanity and the humour and the absurdity in things'.

All of which informed Kalman's deconstruction of the motel sign: a minor incidental object that reveals a sophisticated set of thoughts about security and the profit motive, a deterrent filtered through the language of hospitality. Kalman hopes to 'remind us that we should really be very curious and look around and not take things for granted', he said. **Find the joy in wondering about that toilet paper roll or that coffee cup lid or that onion ring,** and think: "Perhaps this is just as strong a definition of who we are as anything some sociopolitical journal might stamp on us"'.

'It's looking at the big through the small'.

CHANGE *IS* TO *COULD BE*

In an essay that sought to expand the usual thinking about mindfulness, psychologist and writer Adam Grant described a practise he called *conditional thinking* – or 'thinking in conditionals instead of absolutes'. As an example, he pointed to an experiment in which subjects were given a handful of objects and asked to fix an error that had been made in pencil. Each group got the same stuff. For one group the object descriptions were narrow and specific: 'This is a rubber band', and so on. The other group heard slightly different descriptions, subtly ambiguous. For example: 'This could be a rubber band'.

The latter group, Grant explains, was thus gently primed to think conditionally – not to see what *is*, but to see what *could be*. And in the group of conditional thinkers, about 40 per cent realised a rubber band can also be used as an eraser. In the group of absolute thinkers, only 3 per cent had the same epiphany and were able to complete the task.

Grant's riff on conditional thinking reminded me of an acquaintance of mine who calls himself Rotten Apple. He's a designer whose side work includes small-scale but highly creative 'interventions' that transform overlooked urban flotsam into useful or appealing elements

> Change *is* to *could be*, and
>
> you become more mindful.
>
> ADAM GRANT

of the pedestrian environment. For instance, a clip-on seat could turn a bike stand into a chair; discarded chopping boards converted into chess tables could be installed atop fire hydrants; sudoku puzzles could be imposed on underground station tiles; a skipping rope could be made of abandoned construction tape.

Rotten Apple is an amazing conditional thinker. On a casual walk through his neighbourhood, he can reveal exploitable details of bike racks, explain how plastic traffic barriers are weighted by water and stop mid-sentence to collect some stray milk crate or other discard for future use – always noting, in effect, what *could be.*

You don't have to be a street designer to enjoy the benefits of conditional thinking. **Looking for *an* answer instead of *the* answer can shift and broaden your vision.**

DON'T PHOTOGRAPH.DRAW

The smartphone has turned many of us into habitual photographers and everyday documentarians. This familiar development has been widely celebrated and occasionally lamented. However you feel about it, suppose the next time you were tempted to capture a snapshot of an appealing or interesting scene, you drew it instead?

Variations on this idea go back at least to the Victorian-era critic and writer John Ruskin, who was in part reacting to the rise of photography when he argued that the sketcher became a far better observer than the non-sketcher.

Many people, of course, believe that they 'can't draw', meaning that they're not terribly good at drawing and find trying to draw either frustrating or embarrassing. Sometimes I am one of those people.

Be heartened that you don't need to show your drawing to anyone. Get yourself a cheap little notebook and pull it out the next time you're tempted to reach for your phone. Draw one thing – just one! Then do it again. You'll find that drawing helps you slow down and enriches what you see.

Fill your notebook.

The great benefit of drawing . . . is that when you look at something, you see it for the first time. And you can spend your life without ever seeing anything.

MILTON GLASER

DRAW EVERYTHING

Drawing brings forth attention.

The many advocates of 'sketch noting' – a method of note-taking that relies on an improvised combination of thumbnail drawings and highly selective transcription – are quite vocal about the whys and how-tos of their passion for documenting lectures and classes this way.

Carla Diana, a designer and educator, offers an interesting variation on the idea of sketch noting. 'I find that drawing everything in sight as isolated objects – like the conference room speakerphone, the saltshaker, the light switch, etc. – helps me to notice each one better', she said.

Deconstructing almost *any* visual scenario can be revealing. Your desk or your coffee table or your nightstand is likely a jumbled mini-landscape of objects; some shift and move as the days pass, while others are seemingly anchored to their territories. Consider each part separately from the whole. Imagine a series of drawings of each and every thing in your field of vision. Now make that series.

SKETCH A ROOM YOU JUST LEFT

Take in your physical environment carefully, then move to a different one. Now sketch the layout of the room you left. It doesn't need to be a detailed recreation, but strive to capture the basics of the space, including what is in it – the positioning of the doors and windows, for instance, and the footprint of the furniture.

Try it.

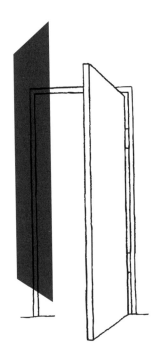

LOOK FOR THE PLOT

When Geoff Manaugh, the author of *A Burglar's Guide to the City,* walks into a bank or a restaurant, he thinks: if a crime was to occur here – a heist, a robbery – who would be involved? That guy who's sitting alone in the corner? The one milling around outside? *What's about to happen here?*

Speculating about what *might* happen next requires a determined focus on key details. Manaugh compares it to a game. Check out the people at a public event: who looks familiar and why? Take in the books on the shelves in a stranger's house: what interests are revealed? When house-hunting in earthquake-prone Los Angeles, Manaugh asked himself: which part of the structure I am looking at – the wood trim, the uneven framing or the loose floorboards – offers a clue about what would collapse first should the worst occur?

Manaugh admits that something about this way of thinking may sound slightly dark. But, he adds:

'I tend to notice things that come in handy later'.

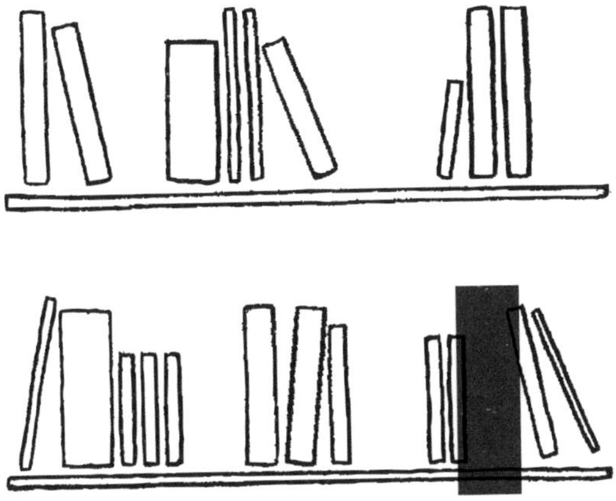

OBSERVE FORCES

Social scientists carefully observe the facts of the world. But that may just be a starting point. 'It's not just about observing what a person does', says Dan Ariely, a professor of psychology and behavioural economics at Duke University and the author of *Predictably Irrational,* among other books. 'It's trying to understand the reasons behind that'.

Ariely's research focuses on how to tweak human behaviour – and that depends on understanding what shapes behaviour in the first place. 'Let's say we go to a bar, and we see people that are dating', Ariely suggests. We also notice that the place is noisy, that it's dark, that it's crowded, that there's alcohol: all sound observations. 'But now, as a social scientist, I want to think of it like a Newtonian physics problem', he continues, 'and say: "What are the *forces* at work? What's pulling people in different directions that is showing up as an interest in being in this place?"'

He offers a few examples: 'Maybe going to a noisy place helps people overcome moments of awkward silence', he says. 'Maybe being in a loud place allows people to sit closer to each other, and from time to time whisper or talk in each other's ear'. Maybe being around a lot of other people offers some sense of safety – but also enough activity to keep one from feeling like the centre of attention. And so forth.

These 'forces' are, strictly speaking, invisible. We're talking about mind-sets and feelings, instincts that even the individuals involved may not be consciously aware of.

Invisible forces are a fun challenge to seek out – particularly in a situation that involves lots of people drawn (or thrown) together, whether at a party or at the Department of Motor Vehicles.

The relation between what we see and what we know is never settled. Each evening we see the sun set. We know that the earth is turning away from it. Yet the knowledge, the explanation, never quite fits the sight.

JOHN BERGER

Try looking like:

A HISTORIAN

A VANDAL

A FUTURIST

A BAD GUEST

∀N IMPROV PERFORMER

A CHILD

LOOK LIKE A HISTORIAN

A few years ago, Matthew Frye Jacobson noticed something simultaneously startling and mundane while walking around Midtown Manhattan. A massive jumbotron-style screen offered a looped image: a young woman, bouncing soft-pornishly on a trampoline and flashing an improbable smile. Titillating or offensive, she was difficult to miss.

What Jacobson, a historian and the chair of American Studies at Yale University, really noticed was how easily we take the likes of Bouncing Jumbotron Woman for granted. He asked his students to consider a photograph of this spectacle. At a glance, they could of course tell that the scene was not from 1930s – or even 1970s – America. They also knew, after a moment of reflection, that there are nations and cultures in the world right now where this scenario couldn't exist.

Jacobson posed a question: what are the preconditions, the things that have to be in place, for this visual to be a casually accepted part of a public environment?

The classroom explored the evolution of technology; shifting personal politics and cultural mores; feminism and antifeminism; varied social norms around sex, advertising and other subjects in different cultures and nation states; the commercialisation of public space; and more. 'There was nothing that I could have told them', Jacobson said, 'that would have been as powerful a lesson'.

Even the most crass intrusion on our attention holds a secret history that hides in plain sight. Deconstruct it. **See the world on your own terms.**

LOOK LIKE A VANDAL

Some of the most imaginative observers of the streetscape I have ever known have been street artists. They examine the built environment with an eye towards detecting the spaces that would be most effective to exploit. I'm particularly drawn to the work of street artists whose creations incorporate and transform urban elements.

Mark Jenkins, for example, once arranged slices of toast in a street vent and on another occasion laid out a red carpet that led right into a sewer opening.

Artist Oakoak, who works in Europe, has an equally clever style, painting figures that seem to interact with crosswalks and traffic barriers and building elements.

Canadian Aiden Glynn adds charming googly eyes to skips, utility boxes and other dull features of the street.

French artist Clet imposes shadowy figures on traffic signs.

I'm not suggesting you *become* a street artist – not everybody wants to risk jail time for creative expression. But it's now easy to examine and enjoy such work from around the world on sites such as Street Art Utopia. And you can be a street artist in your own mind. Steal the street artist's way of seeing. Imagine the streets are your canvas. What would you do with them?

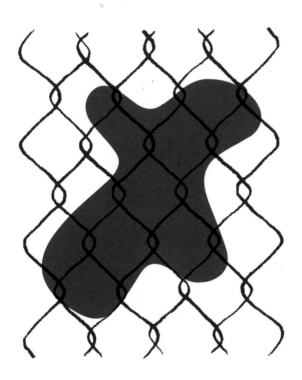

LOOK LIKE A FUTURIST

Rita J. King is a futurist, that most mysterious-sounding of professional categories. She is codirector of a strategic consultancy called Science House, which works with clients from start-ups to fortune 100 companies, helping them position large and ongoing projects for the future. She also contributes her stills to the Science & Entertainment Exchange of the National Academy of Sciences in the US and has worked with NASA, IBM and CBS.

'You can't understand the future unless you understand the patterns that got us here', she says. This means learning about the past and closely observing the present. In particular, she needs an eye for what she calls the 'un-inventable details' that are right in front of us if only we'd attend to them. **'I'm a radical now-ist'**, she says.

Here's a relatively simple exercise she suggests anyone can use. 'Pick a spot, a local park or something, where there are people coming and going', she says. 'Sit there for an hour and write down three things you notice about each person that you see. If there's too many people, just pick one at a time. But just note something. It can be physical or less tangible, like the way their voice sounds or the way they laugh or how their shoulders are hunched or are they wearing a wedding ring. Maybe somebody has a picnic basket for a purse. Whatever'.

You may notice patterns or disruptions of patterns. You may learn something about yourself in what you notice. You may notice something that proves unexpectedly helpful in the future.

LOOK LIKE A BAD GUEST

A friend of mine once told me: 'I'm usually looking for the best way not to be trapped at a place I don't want to be'. I know this feeling well. I've learned how to cope with parties and crowds and other group scenarios that used to make me wildly anxious. But when I walk into those situations, the first thing I do is plot my escape route.

My friend does the same. 'I'll back my truck in and park in a spot where I won't get blocked in when going to social functions I really don't want to be at', he says. 'Or I'll take the seat by the back door and look for all the exits. I'd like to say that there is some Jason Bourne reason and that I'm some kind of badass. But I just get annoyed easily and look for ways to slip out unnoticed. In some weird way, it makes me more observant!'.

If you are anything like my friend or me, you know this intuitively. Next time you're in one of these uncomfortable situations, observe your own observational behaviour – and maybe take a second to laugh at yourself, too.

And if you're *not* like my friend or me: try it out! Spend your next social outing with one eye towards what you would do, how you would move, if you simply *had* to get away, as unnoticed as possible, in five minutes.

LOOK LIKE AN IMPROV PERFORMER

Walking downtown across Union Square in Manhattan one night, Charlie Todd glanced up at the six-storey building at the southern edge of the park. Underused for years, it had lately been living up to its retail promise, fully occupied and bustling thanks to a new Whole Foods on the bottom two floors. What Todd noticed, however, was in one of the windows higher up, in a big clothing store, a young girl dancing.

Lit by the store's fluorescent lights, she was so *visible*. And she seemed to be having a ball. Todd thought, 'That's funny. Why is she doing that'? A few seconds later, another girl appeared and gave the dancer a hug – it must have been a dare or just a silly performance to please a friend. But she had revealed to Todd a de facto stage, in front of a considerable audience. He had an epiphany: 'what I need to do is put someone in every window, dancing'.

Todd is the founder of Improv Everywhere, which is a 'comedy collective that stages unexpected performances in public places'. He had come to New York City in the early 2000s in pursuit of a career as a comic actor and found ways to use the city itself as a venue. One early stunt, the No Trousers underground Ride (the first iteration involved Todd and six other men who boarded the same underground carriage, at different stops, in their boxers, on a cold winter day), has grown into an annual ritual with thousands of participants in dozens of cities. Improv Everywhere has also organised big groups of volunteer strangers to freeze en masse in Grand Central Terminal, burst into song in a department store, dance silently in the park, and so on.

These are amazing feats of logistics and basic human trust; Todd has written a book about Improv Everywhere and the enterprise was the subject of a documentary. But what has always struck me as most impressive about Todd's project is the starting point for each of his ideas and performances – the noticing of some bigger opportunity within an ephemeral human moment. Like spotting a girl dancing for fun in a shop window.

'I think it's taking inspiration from the city', he says. 'Just noticing when there's a new building or there's a new retail store, and being open to seeing the city in a different way'. For a while, Todd taught improv at the famous Upright Citizens Brigade comedy organisation. Maybe the most important thing you can train an aspiring improviser to do, he says, is listen and observe and stay fully open to the possibilities in whatever his or her fellow actors might be saying or doing. Thus the famous 'Yes, and . . .' rule: Whatever your partner says or suggests, you never contradict or disregard it; you embrace it and build on it.

Practise this kind of openness to your environment. Look for flickers of human individuality amid the routine of the everyday. Imagine how that flicker could be amplified and extended, how a fleeting moment can be remade into an unforgettable one. Engage with your world and say, 'Yes! And . . .'

That kind of deep attention that we pay as children

is something that I cherish, that I think we all can

cherish and reclaim, because attention is that

doorway to gratitude, the doorway to wonder,

the doorway to reciprocity. And it worries me greatly

that today's children can recognise 100 corporate

logos and fewer than ten plants.

ROBIN WALL KIMMERER

LOOK LIKE A CHILD

John Berger, in his famous *Ways of Seeing* documentary series and book, relentlessly critiqued visual culture, teasing out secret histories and exposing stealthy biases. It was (and remains) a sophisticated and nuanced take on perception.

But Berger also pointed out that often the most honest, blunt and no-nonsense observers are not highfalutin culture critics. They are children. Not yet having absorbed any particular sense of what is of acceptable cultural interest and what isn't, children see novelty and wonder in the familiar. They notice what we've long since learned to ignore.

'The child sees everything in a state of newness; he is always drunk', Baudelaire wrote. 'Nothing more resembles what we call inspiration than the delight with which a small child absorbs form and colour'; this is the 'genius of childhood – a genius for which no aspect of life has become *stale*'.

The artist Yolanda Dominguez made a short film that I suspect Berger would have loved. She asked children to offer their perspective on high-fashion and luxury-brand imagery. In *Niños vs. Moda* ('Children vs. Fashion'), a group of eight-year-olds are presented with fashion ads and asked to describe what they see. 'She seems . . . scared', a boy offers in reaction to one image. 'She needs a first-aid kit to get healed', a girl says. 'She feels alone', adds another boy. 'And she's hungry'.

Sad as that all sounds, it's also revelatory. Children are blunt and curious and they are effortlessly imaginative and insightful.

We may never be able to recapture exactly the feeling of looking at the world before we'd spent so much time looking at the world. But next time you are confronted with some scene or situation that feels numbingly familiar, stop and ask: what would a child see here?

FIND SOMETHING YOU WEREN'T LOOKING FOR

As a kid, Davy Rothbart walked to and from his school bus stop by way of a sports field where various detritus piled up: sweet wrappers, random papers, rubbish. 'Sometimes I would pick up some note that was blowing in the wind', he later recalled. 'It could be some kid's homework assignment. But it was at least entertaining reading for the rest of my walk home'.

This became a hobby. In college, he enjoyed poking through the abandoned and forgotten leftovers next to the two printers that served hundreds of computers – random email among friends, a highly academic paper about *Friday the 13th,* whatever.

Rothbart's career began with a note he discovered stuck to his windshield late one night in Chicago. It was addressed to Mario.

It said:

Mario, I fucking hate you. You said you had to work. Why is your car here at her place? You're a liar, you're a fucking liar. I fucking hate you. Amber.

Then it said:

PS, page me later.

Rothbart showed the note to friends. 'I was amazed how many of them had great finds to show me in return', he told me. 'Like a kid's drawing or a weird to-do list, a personal note, a Polaroid. People always seemed to have these things taped to their fridge. It seemed like a shame that only the people that wandered into their kitchen would get to see that stuff'.

Rothbart evangelised about the pleasures of the found in what he calls a Johnny Appleseed strategy. He put up flyers looking for others' finds. 'It would give me an excuse to talk to people at parties', he continued. 'You know, "Hey, have you guys ever found something?" Some people would say, "No, you're weird". But a shocking number of people were like, "Yeah, my roommate found something great last week; we'll send it to you"'.

He self-published *Found,* a zine collecting such treasures. This led to books, film projects, an online community. 'It has changed my life', Rothbart said. 'Noticing these little pieces of paper just brought me out of my own head'. Looking at the world, engaging with other people – these are skills that fuel his career as a writer, creator of audio stories for *This American Life* and his own podcast and independent filmmaker. They're also at the heart of the workshops he runs for aspiring audio producers and others.

Finding something can mean 'rescuing it from oblivion', he mused, which is 'kind of a noble act'.

It takes only a moment to stop and pick something up to determine whether it's interesting. 'You'll never know', Rothbart said, 'unless you take a look'.

Put yourself on the lookout for the potentially interesting as you move through the world: on the Tube, at bus stops, on campuses, at work; in bowling alleys, parking lots, even prison yards. Not every discarded napkin or receipt will fascinate, but one in twenty might. The discards of others can be windows into lives you'd never otherwise see – fragments of stories that open us to wonder and curiosity.

2
SENSING

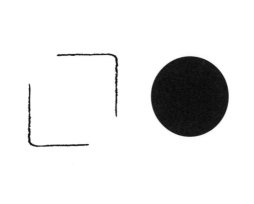

COVER 4'33"

At a 1952 recital in Woodstock, New York, pianist David Tudor gave the premiere performance of an unusual new composition by John Cage. Tudor sat at the piano, placed his sheet music on the music desk – and closed the lid over the keyboard. There he remained, doing nothing. At one point he lifted the lid of the piano and closed it again. Then he repeated that process. And the performance ended.

These three 'movements' added up to four minutes and thirty-three seconds of Tudor's *not playing* the piano. Cage's composition, consisting of a distinct absence of music and thus some mutable combination of silence and incidental noise, was titled 4'33". It is likely his most famous work.

As well it should be.

While it may sound like a prank (and the audience in Woodstock was not impressed), it was the sort of prank that moves a cultural boundary – in this case, the one between what is *music* and what is *silence.* In *Trickster Makes This World,* an excellent book about such acts of disruptive imagination, scholar and writer Lewis Hyde explains that Cage's considered, even disciplined, embrace of chance operations was not just a creative method, but part of an effort to escape his ego.

This piece and its method offer an opportunity anybody can take. You can perform your own cover of 4'33", at home, in the park, or pretty much anywhere else.

Set the timer on your phone for four minutes and thirty-three seconds. Set it to vibrate or chime, place it somewhere screendown and *don't* watch the clock tick. Close your eyes if you can. And just *listen.*

You'll be amazed at how long four minutes and thirty-three seconds feels. Hyde described 4'33" as 'not so much a "silence" piece as a structured opportunity to listen to unintended sound, to hear the plenitude of what happens'. Exactly.

Wherever we are, what we hear is mostly noise.

When we ignore it, it disturbs us.

When we listen to it, we find it fascinating.

JOHN CAGE

FOLLOW THE QUIET

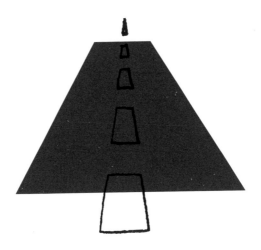

In the PBS Digital Studios series *Art Assignment,* Jace Clayton (also known as DJ /rupture) offered a simple set of instructions.

Go for a walk outside, he advised, but make it a point to head out in the direction that seems the most quiet. Keep going until you find the quietest spot in your vicinity that you can. Now stop and be in that place. 'Take a moment to absorb it', as his instructions put it.

Clayton also suggested you document where you are and upload that documentation to social media with the tag #theartassignment. That's fine, but to me it is not required. Just make sure you really follow through on absorbing what you either hear or don't hear.

MONITOR YOUR SONIC PROFILE

In a brief essay for *The Smart Set* on the subject of noise, writer Bernd Brunner takes note of a woman named Julia Rice. In the early twentieth century, Rice founded the Society for the Suppression of Unnecessary Noise, leading a campaign to force tugboats to cut down their loud whistle signalling. It succeeded.

'However', Brunner points out, 'Rice seems to have enjoyed quite a bit of noise in her life: her six children played instruments and the family allegedly kept a number of cats and dogs. She probably would have classified this as "necessary"'.

Indeed, the difference between sound and noise, let alone *unnecessary* noise, can be subjective. I suspect most of us, like Rice, consider the routine noises we're responsible for in the course of daily life to be not only unobjectionable but, yes, necessary. And maybe we're right. Certainly I don't think I cause any sonic difficulties for anyone else.

On the other hand, what do you really know about your personal sonic profile? **Spend just a few hours or a day monitoring yourself.** Listen to and think about the sounds you make – walking, typing, clearing the dishes, talking, singing along with a favourite tune. Take notes. Experiment with making as little sound as possible and then with making as much sound as possible, and note how this changes your concentration, the way you move, the speed at which you perform routine tasks.

MAKE AN AUDITORY INVENTORY

One of my students began collecting sounds. Before going to sleep, she'd listen intently, striving to pick out and identify every noise. A distant barking dog. The hum of the air conditioner. A passing car.

Applying this idea over time can be a way to rediscover a familiar setting. Collecting at a particular time of day is a useful organising device.

Begin to note sounds consciously.

Build an inventory.

Keep hunting. You'll hear things you'd missed altogether.

REVIEW THE EVERYDAY

My friend Marc Weidenbaum is a music writer, among other things, and he has a very interesting personal ritual. 'I like to review everyday sounds', he explains, 'as if they were commercial music releases'. The whirr of an electric toothbrush, the rattly hum of an old taxi, the moan of a foghorn, the purr of a cat: he'll think up a description of the sound, the context in which it occurred, and 'whatever continuity it's part of (cultural, technological, regional, aesthetic, etc.)', he explains. 'I describe how it functions as a sonic event'. He collects his everyday sound 'reviews' on his site Disquiet.com.

Try this out. Then imagine a version of Yelp built of reviews of everyday things in general – workaday objects, quotidian sounds, unusual sensations, random encounters.

Review a manhole cover or a siren. Review the most interesting thing you touched all week or the most memorable smell you encounter in the next twenty-four hours. Review the very next thing you notice, no matter what it is.

Share your views with a close friend – or keep them to yourself. Do it again tomorrow.

LISTEN SELECTIVELY

Ever listen to the same song over and over again? I bet you have. It's as pleasing as any other binge and it can be instructive. But repeat listening by itself doesn't always get you below the surface of what you've heard before or help you discover what you've never noticed.

Try borrowing from an approach used by Ethan Hein, a musician and educator who teaches music technology at New York University and Montclair State University. Think of it as *critical listening*.

Hein has his students pick a single sound *within* a song, listen for it, and tune out everything else. Maybe it's the bass; maybe it's the vocal. Or maybe this means zeroing in on the chorus and identifying *each* sound within that. Hein makes his students create lists and diagrams of their conclusions. What instrument or piece of gear produced that sound? Who played or programmed it? Why did they play it as they did?

'Just attending to these sounds is enough for casual fans', Hein says. It's less important to identify gear than to land on a subjective description that rings true, such as 'that thing that sounds like a seagull'.

On occasion, musicians have actually made these component parts of songs available as distinct audio objects. They're called *stems*. David Bowie, for instance, released the stems for 'Space Oddity'. After you've heard one in isolation, Hein says, it is easy to follow through the complete version. Look for stems, a cappella versions and similar song chunks from other recordings online. Many are available.

Hein says an ardent Beatles fan he knows had a 'revelatory' experience focusing only on the bass parts of the band's songs, which he thought he'd known through and through. 'Now he has a whole new awareness of how those songs work, which he compared to seeing in colour after a lifetime of black and white'. Selective listening can make that magic possible.

HUNT FOR A SOUND

A student of mine once suggested making a specific effort to listen for one sound in particular: birdsong. For him, this was partly an exercise in connecting with nature in a city. But hunting for a single sound could be even more rewarding in a rural or remote location.

The places we think of as merely 'quiet' are of course filled with sounds, which are just subtle or distant or spread out. You could also search for the *source* of a sound (where exactly are those roosters, anyway?), or if listening this way becomes a habit, refine your target – hunt for a specific species of bird, for instance.

Another student had a similar idea and looked for ambient sounds: sounds that weren't in the foreground, that didn't intrude, but rather those that we'd normally tune out as irrelevant. She cited the minor rustling of a plastic bag caught in a tree. Such incidental noises had been an irritant to her, but actively seeking them out flipped her perception. Instead of trying to tune them out, she collected them.

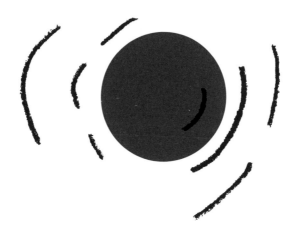

HUNT FOR A FEELING

Ernest Hemingway, in the course of offering his thoughts on just what it is that makes a good writer, complained that most people neither truly listen nor truly observe. To underscore the point, he threw down a gauntlet:

> *You should be able to go into a room and when you come out know*
> *everything that you saw there and not only that. If that room gave*
> *you any feeling you should know exactly what it was that gave you*
> *that feeling. Try that for practise.*

To monitor our surroundings is to focus on what's outside ourselves: what we see, hear, smell, feel and perhaps even taste. But sometimes what really marks a place is something less specific – a *feeling* within us.

An interesting example emerged from a study of underground passenger behaviour. Researchers trying to understand why people sit where they sit or stand where they stand in underground and metro trains scrutinized the factors that shape the way passengers used and navigated that space in different situations. One of their more intriguing findings involved the reasons many passengers like to plant themselves close to the carriage doors. Partly this was the (obvious) convenience of being able to exit more quickly. But partly it was shaped by a more abstract sensation – the desire to avoid 'the sometimes uncomfortable feeling of accidentally making eye contact with seated passengers', according to the researchers' report.

We can't see feelings – but they're very real and they influence our experience of the world. Imagine a map that juxtaposed place and feeling. On a routine trip or a novel exploration, one could make a point to monitor periodically the state of body and mind, a quick-snapshot version of the kind of internal reflection associated with meditation. Where are you uncomfortable or even agitated; where are you carefree with a spring in your step? What are the physical or social influences on that state?

Focus on the final beat of Hemingway's oddly petulant challenge: you notice some feeling within you – anxiety, joy, doesn't matter. Identify the specific sources of that feeling. Later, tell someone about it.

TAKE A SOUND SHOT

Peter Cusack has called his work *sonic journalism,* an auditory equivalent of photojournalism. 'In other words', he once explained, 'getting information from sound recordings of an event or place without too much speech'.

Back in 1998, he started a project called 'Favourite Sounds of London', collecting submissions – short audio clips – from Londoners and posting the results on a dedicated site with a playable map. This has since inspired similar projects from Berlin to Beijing, and most recently Cusack's own favouritesounds.org site has offered a map of favourite sounds of the city of Hull: traffic, playground noise, squawking birds, a band at a fair, a public fountain. Cusack himself has embarked on other projects, notably 'Sounds from Dangerous Places', collecting audio from environmentally damaged sites around the world.

Favourite Sounds asked contributors to both name and explain their entry. But the real goal had less to do with sonic mapping, Cusack explained, than with trying to 'get people talking about the way they hear everyday sounds and how they react to them, or what they think and feel about them, and how important (or not important) they are'. Usually when people talk about where they live, they discuss what part of town they live in and what they do during the day or how they travell. Try thinking instead about what you hear.

'You learn a lot about the city by asking about its sound', he continued. 'And you learn different things about it than if you're asking questions about how it looks, its visual impact. So for me, that's been very interesting. I was sent to new parts of London that I've never heard of before – even though it's my hometown and I know it very well'.

You don't need to participate in an official project to play. Over the course of a day or a month, make a point of using the voice memo app on your phone to take audio snapshots – sound shots, as it were. Think about what you're choosing to record. Listen back to the results and see if you can recall the locales. Play some for a friend and see if he or she can figure out what they are. Talk about where you recorded them and why. Invite your friend to do the same with you.

Expand your attention to include everything

that you can possibly hear, without judgement.

The ear hears. The brain listens.

PAULINE OLIVEROS

LISTEN DEEPLY

The composer Pauline Oliveros was known, among other things, for a practise she called *deep listening*. This evolved in part from her experience performing with a couple of other musicians in an abandoned cistern in the state of Washington, three metres underground. The group shared a weakness for bad puns and titled a 1989 CD of their recordings in the space *Deep Listening*.

But the extraordinary reverb in the cistern really had forced the musicians to listen with deep and extraordinary care to their environment. Thus the performances (there was no audience) prompted them to think in new ways about the relationships between the sonic and the spatial. This led to the Deep Listening Band, Deep Listening workshops and 'retreats', and eventually the Deep Listening Institute. Oliveros later explained that the practise developed into something that 'explores the difference between hearing and listening'.

Hearing is a physical process involving sound waves and the body. We know about it because it is easy to study; listening, the *interpretation* of those sound waves, is harder to quantify.

'To hear is the physical means that enables perception', Oliveros continued. 'To listen is to give attention to what is perceived, both acoustically and psychologically'.

Oliveros's version of listening encompasses remembered sounds, sounds heard in dreams, even imagined or invented sounds. Elsewhere she referred to *auralization* (a term borrowed from architectural acoustics) as a kind of sonic corollary to the visual spin we tend to put on imagination. 'Listening is a lifetime practise that depends on accumulated experiences with sound', she asserted, one that encompasses 'the whole space-time continuum of sounds'.

Well before arriving at the term *deep listening*, Oliveros had experimented with many of these ideas and notably produced a short but influential 1974 text called *Sonic Meditations*, offering various sets of rather poetic instructions:

'Take a walk at night'.

'Walk so silently that the bottom of your feet become ears'.

Most of the highly inventive prompts also involve making sounds, particularly in groups, consistent with her belief that musicality shouldn't be restricted to musicians. For example, 'Choose a word. Listen to it mentally. Slowly and gradually begin to voice this word by allowing each tiny part of it to sound extremely prolonged. Repeat for a long time'.

You can piece together and modify some of Oliveros's suggestions to explore deep listening without worrying about compositional goals. Here is one approach to experimenting with the kind of expansive listening that she advocated, borrowing from a few sources, but most notably a 'meditation' that was part of a 2011 Deep Listening Intensive in Seattle. Think of this as a means of exploring your aural identity:

In any space you wish, 'listen to all possible sounds'. When one sound grabs your attention, dwell on it. Does it end? Think about what it reminds you of. Consider sounds from your past, from dreams, from nature, from music.

Now think of a sound that reminds you of childhood; see if you can find something reminiscent of that sound now. Dwell on what you find. Stop here or follow the instruction of that 2011 meditation for as long as you wish: 'Return to listening to all sounds at once. Continue in this manner'.

MAKE A SOUND MAP

As part of a course on sound in the media landscape at the Academy of Art University in San Francisco, writer Marc Weidenbaum – I mentioned him in the earlier item on reviewing the everyday – takes his students on a *soundwalk*. This is a walking tour of sounds rather than sights. One such tour began in a Market Street mall, taking in the retail soundtrack. Then it headed outside and moved east on a route punctuated by street chatter, traffic noise and the occasional siren; paused outside the lobby of an exclusive residential building offering 'private silence'; considered the auditory effects of the waterfall feature of a Martin Luther King Jr. memorial; and got interrupted by a street evangelist bellowing through a megaphone.

Students learn to notice not just how sounds work but also where they come from and when and why.

Weidenbaum instructs students to identify three sounds in a two-block radius and to 'pin' each sound's origin point on a digital map, describing it and noting its meaning or function.

Even a purely hypothetical version of such a map presents some helpful questions. Should it include the ephemeral and unmoored sounds of a passing bird's squawk, an airplane, distant thunder? Or should it stick to more geographically immobile examples: a church bell, a penned rooster, the warning horn of a drawbridge?

As an extra-credit assignment, Weidenbaum encourages his students to chart a soundwalk of their own, designing it around a particular theme with multiple audible points of interest. The result is a 'narrated journey', as he puts it, addressing 'the sonic aspects (be they aesthetic, cultural, historical, functional, etc.)' of a place.

'The world is a museum', he says. 'You are the docent'.

MAKE A SENSORY MAP

Think of a map as something that documents and organises more than sights and places. Expand your thinking even beyond sound to touch and taste.

Collect tactile sensations, toggling between a focus on the things you naturally touch and touching things you normally wouldn't. Note what's rough or smooth, warm or cool, hard or soft. 'I like to take a moment to notice what things feel like by tapping, poking, stroking and scratching', Carla Diana, the designer and drawing enthusiast I mention earlier, once told me. 'It makes me appreciate the way things move around, like M&Ms in a bag, or variations in temperature, like the coolness of a bicycle tube, or the direction of a fabric's fibres, or the roughness of brick as you're walking by a wall'.

That's a great way to think as you experience the world. Contrast the natural and the human-made. Take inspiration from the title of the legendary architecture critic Ada Louise Huxtable's most famous book: *Kicked a Building Lately?*

Taste is admittedly more of a challenge – I can't endorse *licking* a building – but it's not impossible. Be alert to sources of the (safely) edible around you, from the fruit tree to the vending machine. Map the tastes that define a block, a neighbourhood, a town.

TAKE A SCENT WALK

Observation of smell has inspired a number of compelling works and projects that can in turn inspire us to figure out better ways to follow our noses, as it were.

Victoria Henshaw, a British scholar, urban planner and author of the 2013 book *Urban Smellscapes,* devoted her career to the subject. Her practise included organising *smellwalks* in Sheffield, and elsewhere, drawing on her research into 'contemporary experiences of odours in town and cities'. The Henderson's Relish factory was a centrepiece of the walk in Sheffield.

As she recounted in one interview, it wasn't necessarily the routes of her smellwalks that were remarkable, but the simple fact of prompting participants to focus explicitly on scents and odours – which they often reported were familiar in that I-know-this-but-I-never-thought-about-it way. 'We'd walk through an area, and because I was asking them to focus on smell', she once explained, 'they would say things like, "You know, that smell *is* very familiar – I smell it every day and I really like it, but I've not consciously registered that it was there before – I've just whizzed past"'.

Artists Kate McLean and Sissel Tolaas have also used scent and smell as tools for discovery, exploration and understanding. Tolaas, a Norwegian based in Berlin, has worked regularly with International Flavors & Fragrances (IFF), which develops scents for luxury brands. She spent years amassing a 'smell archive', stored in thousands of airtight jars and has conducted more than fifty city smellscape projects in London, Istanbul, Tokyo, Calcutta, Auckland and elsewhere.

In Kansas City, she 'collected' smells from six neighbourhoods in the city, on both sides of the Missouri/Kansas border, using a portable funnel-and-tube device borrowed from IFF. These scents were then embedded in scratch-and-sniff cards and made available at distribution points around the city as an exploratory game.

McLean, who is British, has made smellmaps of Amsterdam, Edinburgh, Milan, New York and other cities. In Amsterdam, she took multiple walks with dozens of locals, working with them to identify eleven core smells that 'represent' the city and plotting the locations where one might experience them. Sometimes she focuses on details of some more micro smellscape: the way retailers' open doors have an olfactory effect on a portion of a single city block, for instance.

And of course McLean's work confronts *bad* smells, investigating, for instance, the 'smelliest blocks' of New York City, and the various combinations of stagnant water, dried fish and cabbage.

McLean offers a handy PDF guide for conducting your own smellwalk at sensorymaps.com/about. (She calls this a smellfie kit.) I'll quote here some of the basics:

- Be alert for curious and unexpected smells, but also for 'episodic' smells specific to a particular area – flowers or cooking, let's say – and background smells that are less intense but suggest an olfactory 'context'.

- Walk slowly and note at least four distinct smells; she calls this relatively passive approach *smell catching*. Write them down, noting the location, the smells' intensity and duration and your own reaction and thoughts.

- Try *smell hunting* – crushing leaves, for instance, or actively sniffing at a wall or other object – and note four more.

- Collect four final smells using either method described; discuss your findings with fellow smellwalkers, if appropriate. Choose a smell that 'summarises the area'.

My job is really to pay attention and

see what's there that we haven't

seen yet. I'm always trying to look

at the things we are overlooking and

underestimating in terms of their

interest or value.

NINA KATCHADOURIAN

NOTICE WHAT YOU NOTICED (AND DIDN'T)

Notice something you always notice; now notice something you've *never* noticed. This is a provocation that the artist Nina Katchadourian has given students in the past, and while it sounds simple, it can be revelatory.

Katchadourian 'performs curiosity', as one observant critic puts it. She created the thirty-minute audio tour of the Museum of Modern Art's dust that I mentioned earlier. Another project involved equipping a 'flock' of cars with alarms of birdcalls, which had been modified to fit a standard six-tone alarm-sound structure.

Perhaps her best-known ongoing project is called 'Seat Assignment'. In 2010, Katchadourian was faced with a seemingly endless series of flights that trapped her in the profoundly uninspiring space of an airline seat. She resolved that she would henceforth require herself to use that time to create a work of art entirely with materials ready to hand. Since then she's created hundreds of photographs, a number of videos and animations and more, all by scrutinising and manipulating familiar objects in her immediate proximity.

The results are delightful, including a bunch of somewhat surreal images made by, say, piling bread crumbs on a picture from an in-flight magazine or wafer snacks documented at an angle that makes them curiously resemble the original twin World Trade Center towers. And in an even more remarkable variation, she achieves the promise of her Lavatory Self-Portraits in the Flemish Style subset of 'Seat Assignment' images entirely by manipulating disposable towels and other available paper products to resemble the sombre and fussily costumed subjects of fifteenth-century portraiture.

As writer Jeffrey Kastner observed: **'Attention to the world is the proper vocation not just of the artist but of anyone who imagines it as a place worthy of preservation'.**

That's why the prompt Katchadourian gave her students can help us pay better attention to the world. You might do something similar within some familiar place: the streets around your office, a room you regularly spend time in, a public space you visit often. Katchadourian asked students to document each thing they notice and explain their findings – and in one instance organised a group walking tour of each item her students had chosen.

The contrast between what's caught your attention and what hasn't can be instructive. Just take a half hour, anywhere and really **notice what you notice.** Sometimes what we need is the confidence to believe that what we notice actually matters: After all, if nobody else ever mentions it, we might think it's just not that important. Get over that feeling. It's precisely the stuff everybody else has missed that ought to make us think twice. *Why* do you always notice this and why doesn't anyone else seem to?

CHANGE THE SCALE

In 1977, the famous husband-and-wife design duo Charles and Ray Eames completed the final version of a nine-minute film called *Powers of Ten,* dealing with 'the relative size of things in the universe'.

It begins with an overhead view of a couple picnicking in a Chicago park. The narrator explains that the shot is one metre wide, viewed from one metre away. Every ten seconds, he continues, the view will pull back by a factor of ten: a view ten metres wide, from ten metres away, then 100 metres, then 1,000 and so on. The couple quickly disappears; our view is citywide, then nationwide, then includes the entire Earth. By 10^8 metres, we're firmly in outer space. The journey stops at 10^{25} metres – the size of the known universe – before reversing course. Zooming quickly back down to the couple, it keeps going, this time zooming in on the man's hand and into the realm of subatomic particles, concluding at 10^{-18} metres.

Apart from inspiring the closing shot of the first *Men in Black* movie, the Eameses' film offered a vivid lesson in scale, how we measure it and experience it. Years later, their grandson Eames Demetrios organised a *Powers of Ten* exhibit at the California Academy of Sciences. 'Scale is like geography', he observed at the time. 'If you don't know where Afghanistan is when you hear it mentioned in the news, you won't have a place to hang it in your mind. Numbers are the same. Anthrax is measured in microns; pesticide residues are reported in parts per billion. These numbers are important to our lives – we should be able to understand what they mean'.

Take a fresh look at any environment. Pause to change scale by focusing on *details*; maybe use your phone's camera zoom to heighten what your eyes can perceive. Now stop and think about the 'big picture' – about where you are in a scale you can't see yourself but can only imagine.

CHANGE THE (TIME) SCALE

◉

Scale is a physical idea, but it is also a temporal one.

Look for the oldest thing around you. It might be a particular building on a street, a specific object within a room, a tree in a landscape. The answer may be obvious or impossible to determine with certainty.

Now look for the newest thing around you.

Consider what the venerable and the recent have in common – and what sets them apart.

Consider which will outlast the other and why.

IMBUE YOUR WORLD WITH GOD SPIRITS

I'm not quite sure how to describe my friend Lucian James – perhaps as some kind of combination of performance coach, spiritual adviser and strategic consultant? He's someone I check in with whenever I'm looking for an original point of view about . . . pretty much anything. I knew if I asked him about noticing and attention, he'd have something to say.

'There are two types of religions in the world, transcendent and immanent', his reply began. 'The former are religions that typically grew up in desert surroundings where God is seen as living above and beyond, "sky god" religions. The latter are religions that grew up in forest surroundings where God is seen as living inside all things, pagan, folk religions'. It was the latter he wanted me to consider, specifically Japanese Shinto practises.

Westerners, he told me, often see Shinto adherents as exhibiting a 'kind of stylized reverence toward everything'. So James teaches his clients that 'they can borrow that and do a kind of daily Shinto practise toward everything and everyone they come across.'

We can imbue 'everything with a little god spirit. So my laptop has a little god inside it. So does this cup of water. So do my shoes. Et cetera'.

This might sound a bit mystical. But although James frames it in the context of religion, finding the 'god spirit' doesn't actually require any particular religious orthodoxy – or really, any religious faith at all.

Just pause over, let's say, some object you happen to be in contact with right now. A stapler on your desk, for instance. Consider what 'little god' might reside within it, and what that might mean. 'It's strange', James told me, 'that instantly people know exactly how to do it. They start treating everything – pens, shoes, food – in a more "everyday sacred" kind of way'.

Or perhaps it's not so strange at all.

Practise a Shinto-influenced Buddhist take on noticing by maintaining 'a single point of concentration'. That's seemingly a straightforward proposition – and yet, as James observed, 'all of contemporary culture conspires against our ability to do this'. Focus on one thing and search for the 'sacred' within it.

Even in one single leaf on a

tree, or in one blade of grass,

the awesome deity presents itself.

SHINTO SAYING

TRY A MENTAL PALATE CLEANSER

When I was in my twenties and was working way too many hours a week, I was still determined to have a life outside my job. So I signed up to attend a weekly documentary series. Predictably, it was a challenge to make time for this. The night of the third screening, I was in a desperate scramble to get to the venue on time and arrived just as the lights were going down, too distracted to remember what the film would be and too busy to check. I flopped into the seat and on flickered – *Triumph of the Will.* Great. Just what I needed after a day of sensory overload: an overwhelming dose of Nazi bombast and Hitler's screaming.

I was reminded of this ridiculous experience when I learned of artist Marina Abramović's *Goldberg.* In theory, the main event was a performance of Bach's *Goldberg Variations* as played by Igor Levit. But to some extent the real attraction was the prelude. Attendees were required to arrive thirty minutes before the show and sit silently in the venue, wearing noise-cancelling headphones. This was a sort of mental palate cleanser.

Abramović may be best known for her performance *The Artist Is Present,* which involved her showing up at the Museum of Modern Art in New York and sitting across from patrons, one at a time. For as long as they wanted, Abramović sat and the two would silently regard each other. She has also devised a series of exercises called the Abramović Method, which involves focusing on one particular action as a recurring theme. The Abramović Method workshops include activities such as a period of silently regarding another attendee or walking incredibly slowly across a room. Other exercises involve drinking a glass of water with such deliberation and concentration that it takes as long as twenty minutes; spending a full ten minutes writing out your name a single time; and counting every grain in a huge pile of rice. Elsewhere, Abramović has underscored the importance of solitude by declaring that an artist should 'stay for long periods of time' at waterfalls, fast-running rivers and (rather more improbably) erupting volcanoes, as well as taking lengthy looks at the horizon and at the stars in the night sky.

Intriguing as all of these suggestions may be, I'm drawn back to the way Abramović applied her thinking about attention to that *Goldberg* performance. How routinely do you find yourself arriving *just in time* for a significant performance or event or meeting, distractions trailing you like a cloud of dust? Whatever the pros or cons of *Triumph of the Will*, I should have admitted to myself that night that I was not up to giving it authentic attention, walked out and sat in quiet for two hours instead.

Try recreating the spirit of Abramović's *Goldberg* in regular life. Next time you have a dinner out planned with someone you care about, arrive (or plant yourself nearby) early. And do nothing. Observe the world; think about the person you're about to see; cleanse your mental palate of other obligations or distractions.

A significant moment deserves a considered prelude. Be ready.

PRACTISE DIGITAL SILENCE

When we complain about digital devices, we are complaining about the distractions and interruptions inflicted on us by others. That's what we're avoiding when we decide to 'unplug' for a few days.

But is it really always about *other people's* posts and updates? What about your own urge to wave at whatever far-flung audiences you've assembled to remind them that you exist?

Consider observing an occasional week of digital silence.

You are allowed to check the various feeds you follow and monitor online conversations and connections as much as you wish. But do not contribute.

See how this affects your urge to 'connect'. See if it changes your own standards about what you need to communicate and why. I've often wondered what we would see if Facebook or Twitter or Instagram enforced such limits – if we were allowed only three updates a month, let's say. Or what if we could instant message just two people per week? Would this make us restrict ourselves to saying only what really mattered? Would our 'networks' appreciate that?

Would you?

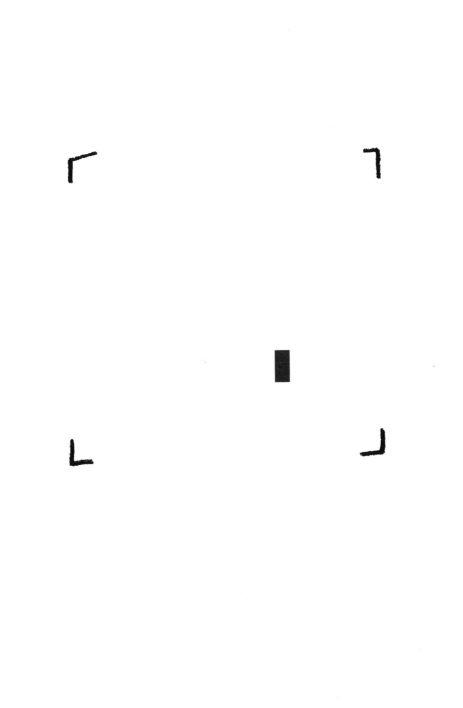

HUNT THE INFRATHIN

Everybody knows that human beings have five senses: vision, audition, gustation, olfaction and somatosensation – better known as sight, hearing, taste, smell and touch.

But that's not really the whole story. You don't have to touch an open flame to feel its heat. That's because of another sense called *thermoception,* the ability to detect temperature differences.

Close your eyes and bring your finger *almost* to your nose. Again, there's no touch involved, but you can sense where your finger is. This is called *proprioception,* our sense of bodily spatial relations.

Other senses include *nociception* or the detection of pain; *equilibrioception*, a sense of balance; and *mechanoreception* or response to a mechanical stimulus such as vibration – a particularly handy thing to discern in the smartphone era, actually. We have a *sense of time. Hunger* is a sense of sorts. Depending on how you define the term, you could argue that humans actually have dozens of senses.

Trying to figure ways to explore our non-obvious senses can be a little daunting. But perhaps Marcel Duchamp can help. In what seems to be one of the lesser known of his many provocations, he introduced a term that seemed important to his work and that he toyed with but never truly articulated, making it a thing easier to offer examples of than to define. The term was *infrathin.* Here's one example of the infrathin offered by Duchaump: *the warmth of a seat that has just been vacated.*

Jay D. Russell, in a paper on the subject, took a shot at a definition: 'The infrathin is, in general, a separation, a difference between two things'. I don't find that terribly satisfying, but let's hang on to it for the moment.

Kenneth Goldsmith, the artist and poet, offers various other examples. The swoosh sound of email being sent is infrathin. The smell of a mouth that has just released tobacco smoke. The heat of paper just emerged from a laser printer. 'Another example might be that when I take a picture on my iPhone, it makes the sound of a Nikon camera from the 1940s or something', Goldsmith suggests. 'That's an interesting moment'. He calls the infrathin 'a state between states'.

Maybe Duchamp was right and it's better to avoid defining the infrathin. It seems to name something that defies naming, artifacts of our perception that fall outside our usual categories of perception.

Hunt for those moments and don't worry about how they might be defined. Trust that if you think you've identified one, you have.

3

GOING PLACES

LOOK FOR GHOSTS AND RUINS

👁 👁

As part of a project overseen by William Cronon, a professor of history, geography and environmental studies at the University of Wisconsin at Madison, a group of graduate students set out to create online resources for environmental history research. Their guide 'How to Read a Landscape' offers many useful suggestions for readers, explorers and researchers. My favourites involve looking for ghosts and ruins. The guide explains:

'Ghost landscapes, are clues left behind from the past that show what a previous landscape may have looked like and how it was altered to achieve its present state. They can be as noticeable as the remnants of an abandoned highway (i.e. Route 66 across the American West or stretches of Route 38 in California) or as unnoticeable as varied growth patterns in trees – which can signify recent planting or, if grown in parallel lines, traces of an abandoned road'.

Ruins are similar: 'the faded records of the past still apparent on the landscape'. An old out-of-service pay phone, for instance, is a ruin. It says something about its own environment and surroundings. The *persistence* of a ruin can also be instructive. Why hasn't someone torn that old pay phone down and hauled it away? Because of its historic significance? Or simply as a function of neglect?

Nobody is making an effort to direct your attention to the ghosts or ruins in any given landscape. But if you want to understand a place more deeply, these are exactly the things you should look for.

Hunt for:

AMBIENT SOUNDS

FEELINGS

PATTERNS

SHAPES

COLOURS

NUMBERS

WINDOWS

GHOSTS

THE MOON

SOMETHING YOU DIDN'T KNOW YOU WERE
LOOKING FOR

THE INFRATHIN

STAND

The 'Standing with Saguaros' project was pretty much what it sounds like. Participants headed to Saguaro National Park outside Tucson, Arizona, to stand for an hour in the proximity of one of the iconic cacti there. (They could also sit and the hour length was more of a suggestion.) About three hundred people actually carried out this exercise.

These participants described connecting with the landscape, appreciating and re-evaluating the familiar cactus, achieving a natural calmness. 'It teaches you patience', one participant, a high school student, commented. 'Time flies by'.

You may not be able to find a saguaro in your vicinity, but when looking for ways to connect with nature or when you're on a long walk or a hike, pick *one* thing – maybe something deceptively familiar, as the saguaro might be to southwestern Americans – and really attend to it.

This idea almost parodies the nature walk. Call it a nature linger, a nature loiter, a nature loaf.

TAKE A PHOTO WALK, WITH NO CAMERA

Googling can lead you to any number of articles and lists with basic suggestions for taking better pictures. I'll choose one: a video that blog pioneer Jason Kottke once posted, appealingly called *23 Ninja Tips for Your Next Photo Walk*. It featured street photographer Thomas Leuthard walking around Salzburg, offering viewers 'potential approaches to being creative with a camera'.

Some of these tips are purely technical. But a number have more to do with spotting a great picture and thus can be employed *without* a camera – as ways to filter the world, notice new things and appreciate them.

Find an interesting backdrop and wait for a compelling subject to wander into it, the video advises; you're looking for a 'decisive moment', and it may take a while to occur. Photographer Eric Kim calls this *fishing*. Camera-free, you can still pause or sit in a particular spot, look around, carefully imagining the pictures you *could* take and wait for the 'right' or 'decisive' moment. When you decide you've seen it, move on to a new spot.

'Find new angles', the video advises, showing Leuthard placing his camera on the ground and perching himself on a bollard. 'Get down low, and up high'. This is solid advice. As you take your camera-free photo walk, take a moment now and again to squat down (pretend you're tying your shoe if you're embarrassed) or step up onto something and consider the view. Imagine taking a snapshot and then continue on your way.

'Look for natural frames for your subjects', the video suggests, offering up an image of women on a park bench, 'framed' by elements of a public sculpture; a composition that places a man typing away at his laptop neatly between two large potted plants and so on. 'Alleys and doorways are great for this', it adds. 'Just duck in and wait'. Here, too, you can deploy these ninja tips without worrying about recording a beautifully composed image. Duck into that alley and wait. When you've seen the right scene, you're done. Keep going.

'Squint your eyes to see the luminance of a scene and place your subject in the brightest spot'. This is a delightful tip, particularly because you can do the first part without worrying about the second. Use this tactic intermittently whenever you notice the light is tricky or interesting.

'Shadows also make great pics. And reflections, too'. Agreed: Make it a point to look out for them.

And finally, 'Don't be afraid of people', the video reassures us. Fair enough, but you can skip the photographer's further step of approaching every interesting human you notice and offering a business card. Instead, you need do no more than smile politely – or wear sunglasses, so your subjects don't know they've been 'captured' by your attention.

WALK WITH AN EXPERT

Solitude can be an excellent state for honing one's attention. But sometimes the right companion can help. Alexandra Horowitz's *On Looking* documents her experience walking around her own neighbourhood with a series of 'experts' – on typography, plant life, public space, geology and so on. While they walked what she thought of as highly familiar territory, Horowitz discovered that her guides were only too happy to help her see the world their way and draw attention to all that was obvious to them yet invisible to her.

We can't all persuade world-famous experts or even locally famous experts, to kill an afternoon meandering around some area of our choosing. But it's not all that hard to find an informal neighbourhood historian (a know-it-all neighbour), one who would be more than happy to expound at length on the secret significance of this house or that area park and the story behind it.

So call the bluff of your neighbour who is forever alluding to your neighbourhood's little-known history. Or flatter the one who happens to be better versed in, say, botany than you are. Walk together and allow your attention to be directed by others; explore your familiar world through an unfamiliar perspective.

> If it catches you sneaking out,
>
> boredom will try to talk you into taking your phone.
>
> If you do, you'll be taking boredom with you.
>
> LYNDA BARRY

DETECT IMAGINARY CLUES

The artist Lynda Barry writes an occasional advice column for the website of *The Paris Review*. She once gave an interesting answer to an unusual question about staving off boredom. Specifically, an inquisitor identified as Tipsy in Texas wanted to know how to entertain oneself without 'drinking too much'.

Barry begins her response by directing the reader straight to the bar. 'Get a ride to one', she advises, 'that's a good walking distance from your home. Don't bring your phone. Get slightly tipsy and head homewards on foot'.

'But before you start your trek home', she advises, 'think of a question, 'big or small', you'd like answered. As you begin to walk home (possibly getting a little lost along the way as you are tipsy and phoneless)', she writes, 'tell yourself that you will encounter three clues to the answer to this question in the next ninety minutes. Tell yourself one will be in the form of a person, one will be in the form of trash or something laying on the ground and one will be something located above eye level'.

Barry's full suggested exercise involves writing when you get home: what happened, what you saw, how it answers your question. Whether you do that (or even whether you actually get tipsy) or not, follow the basic framework. Come up with a question and use some variation of Barry's parameters – maybe adjusted to the environment you'll be travelling – to seek three 'clues' to its answer.

Perhaps Barry's advice really will result in an answer to your question. Whatever the outcome, it's likely to be unpredictable. 'In less than two hours you'll have a big experience that boredom won't know anything about because it's still on your phone', she promises. Even if you write out your findings, she adds:

'Boredom can't read your handwriting'.

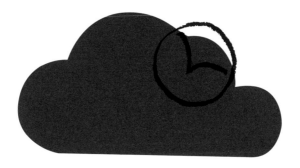

TAKE A LONG WALK THROUGH AN UNFAMILIAR PART OF TOWN

You don't have to travell to the other side of the world to find a new place to explore. Look at a map of your hometown or city and consider the territories you know absolutely nothing about. And then plot yourself a nice long walk.

This strategy of making a preplanned effort to change your surroundings was inspired by Matt Green's project 'I'm Just Walkin'', which documents the systematic wanderings of a man who has set out to walk every single street in New York City. Later, I became familiar with a City College of New York sociology professor named William Helmreich – who *also* walked every street of the city over a period of four years and wrote a book about it: *The New York Nobody Knows*.

This exercise is all about expectations. You are unlikely to discover world historical monuments and famous points of interest. It's the more modest, everyday details you want to seek, absorb and enjoy – a creatively painted shop sign, a stray game of chess, a random but appealing church, a surprising parked vintage car, a passerby who happens to be on a unicycle, etc.

RANDOMISE YOUR MOVEMENTS

◉ ◉ ◉

Max Hawkins, who describes himself as an artist and computer scientist, quit his job at Google and spent two years experimenting with how to randomise how and where he spent his time.

First, he created a personal app that would take him on an Uber journey to a spot, within a preset radius, chosen by his app. Then he made a tool that searched nearby events on Facebook and randomly picked which ones he should attend. 'Once Max explained how and why he had arrived at these events, hosts usually welcomed him, often with only a few questions asked', National Public Radio reported. 'One night he got to drink White Russians with some Russians. Another, he attended acroyoga (as in, acrobatics + yoga). A community centre pancake breakfast. A networking event for young professionals. The algorithm chose; Max attended'.

Over time Hawkins let his algorithms direct where he ate, travelled and (he claims) even lived. Eventually he settled down and made his life less random, but created a Facebook group and public tool called the Third Party to help others find randomly selected Facebook events.

While Hawkins's approach to randomisation seems extreme, the spirit is inspiring. Here's a low-tech alternative: flip a coin.

Any journey will feel a little more adventurous if you add chance to the decision-making process when resolving which restaurant to sample or which direction to turn. And let's face it, sometimes all the worry and study that go into a fully researched and informed decision aren't really worth it.

Just be straight-up random once in a while.

BE A LOCAL TOURIST

Lots of cities and towns have official tours; locals instinctively dismiss them as superfluous, hokey or both. Set that prejudice aside and take the official tour of wherever it is you live. You may learn something about your hometown, and you will certainly learn something about how it's being presented to others – and how they perceive it.

You'll consider a place that is familiar to you, but through the wide and curious eyes of a newcomer.

GET THERE THE HARD WAY

◉ ◉ ◉

Google Maps and its competitors are designed to ease your passage through the world, to guide you turn by turn, step by step, from wherever you are to wherever you say you want to be. As somebody from Google once put it: 'No human ever has to feel lost again'.

I'm sure that Googler meant well, but I find that sentiment chilling. In fact, I'm tempted to suggest 'getting lost' as an explicit goal.

But if that's too extreme, then *risk the possibility* of feeling lost – at least every so often. Next time you're going somewhere new, skip the apps. Study the route in advance by looking at a map – even a digital one. You can bring a printed map along or write the directions down or simply memorise them, but make your journey without any real-time digital guidance. If the trip is a hassle, with wrong turns or false starts, that's good.

Thinkers from Ralph Waldo Emerson to John Dewey have extolled the value of overcoming obstacles to achieve something. This is one simple way to do that.

Get there the hard way: by engaging with the world, not skimming over it.

MISUSE YOUR TOOLS

We shape our tools, the saying goes, and thereafter they shape us.

And maybe they do, if you let them. But one of the most effective ways to remind yourself that you rule your tools, not the other way around, is to *mis*use them.

Many of my students try to solve my challenge to 'practise paying attention' by resorting to their smartphones or other technology. This sounds a little dispiriting, but the good news is that they get much more creative than I ever could in discovering overlooked things this digital tool can do.

One student figured out that most digital map tools include a compass. She used the compass's needle to orient her gaze. Wherever she walked, she'd periodically take a look towards true north, and whatever happened to be there 'introduced a degree of randomness into what I saw'.

COMPILE AN ITINERARY

Hitchhiking from London to the Pyrenees and back sounds pretty exciting. And it seems likely that British artist Hamish Fulton had a memorable adventure when he took just such a trip as a young art student in April 1967. The document that he produced at the journey's conclusion, however, is curiously mundane. The two typewritten pages that he dryly titled 'Hitchhiking Times from London to Andorra and Andorra to London, 9–15 April 1967' consist entirely of bare-bones entries along the lines of *Petrol Station on Route N20 to Orleans, 10 p.m.*

In compiling this anti-travelogue, Fulton had to attend to his travels in a specific way, documenting details of movement we'd normally forget, even if they amount to the very backbone of any given trip. His deadpan document later appeared in a major exhibition at the Tate Britain gallery, where it was explained as describing 'a direct and particular engagement with the world', albeit one in a distinctly minimal form: **'The viewer is left with their own imagination and experiences to expand on what this data may point to'.**

This can be adapted to any history of personal movement – an adventure like Fulton's or just a routine week. Consider a stark, just-the-facts form of journaling, simply noting the beginning and end points of journeys – home to the gym, the gym to the post office, the post office to work, etc. See how this changes the way you think about those journeys, and revisit your journal of movement from time to time.

If you already know how to solve a problem using a tried and true method, avoid doing so. You never know what you'll find along an unfamiliar route.

JIM COUDAL

CHANGE YOUR ROUTE

Let's say you go to work every day. Let's say you know the best way to get there. Let's say that this is the way you always go. Makes sense!

But stop it. At least sometimes. Go out of your way to go out of your way, advises Jim Coudal, whose firm Coudal Partners is known for creative design projects and products, including the famous Field Notes notebook brand.

'On foot, on bike, or in a car – take a different route to a common destination', he says. 'If you commute the same way every day, you don't notice anything. In fact, a few minutes after arriving, you have absolutely no recollection of the journey at all. By going into this zombie commuter state you are actually stealing time from yourself. New routes make for more active and curious journeys'.

'This is an apt metaphor for the creative process too', Coudal adds. Maybe you already know what works – and that's exactly why you should try something different.

DRIFT

The Lettrist International was a collective of radical artists and theorists in 1950s Paris, whose members included Guy Debord. Debord laid down a definition of a practise the group endorsed, called *derivé,* or 'the drift'. It was, in short, a philosophy of movement:

> *One or several persons, giving themselves over to the drift for a period of variable length, dispense with the usual reasons for moving about, and with their relationships, jobs and leisure activities, in order to let themselves follow the pull of the landscape and the encounters that come from it.*

This is a romantic-sounding goal – but also one that's a bit mushy. The writer Luc Sante once offered a theory for where this idea came from that clarifies what it means in practise. Both *derive* and the not-unrelated term 'psychogeography', Sante explained, found their way into the Lettrist vocabulary after the publication, in 1952, of *Paris Vagabond.* Written by a man who called himself Jean-Paul Clébert, it's a memoir of sorts, 'primarily concerned with all the ways in which people managed to survive in the city on no money at all' Sante writes, 'a way of life shared by Clébert himself'.

Clébert drifted in a city where, after the end of the Second World War, many economic structures had crumbled. Finding a way to get by in their absence defined the days of many formerly secure citizens who now 'drifted' because they had no other choice. Clébert took notes, Sante adds, 'with any available pencil on any available paper, such as restaurant placemats and bits of newspaper', and wrote his book by drawing on these scraps at random, making *Paris Vagabond* itself the product of a 'Dada chance operation'.

Borrowing a practise born of necessity, Debord essentially revised it into a kind of aspiration. If you think about it, the connections between money and movement are pretty overwhelming. What happens if you sever them?

Spend a day off travelling your hometown without spending a penny. Spend an afternoon of your holiday in a new city the same way. Clébert (and other writers who preceded or followed him in similar projects) experienced and produced a kind of portrait of the penniless and marginal corners of a city. But just see what happens when you take money out of the equation, however briefly. How does it change where you move, what you look for, how you orient yourself?

Find out what it's like to drift.

TURN A DEPARTMENT STORE INTO A PLAYGROUND

In his book *Play Anything,* technologist and game designer Ian Bogost describes dragging his young daughter through a mall and suddenly realising that while he was focused on completing his various necessary tasks and errands, she had made a game of avoiding stepping on the boundaries of the shopping centre's square tiles. Of course, there's nothing particularly shocking about that. Children don't need to be told that they can convert almost anything into a game or an amusement. They just do it.

Part of Bogost's goal is to help adults think that way, too. Learn to spot new and unintended possibilities, the hidden potentials within existing forms and limits – and play them. Bogost suggests treating Walmart as a playground.

> Pay close, foolish, even absurd
>
> attention to things.
>
> IAN BOGOST

Like Bogost, I visit my local Walmart more often than I'd like to and there's generally nothing fun about it. Picking up the few items I need in the store's fluorescent-lit sprawl always seems to involve hiking past mountains of junk that I don't want. Bogost's insight was that this was a good opportunity to pay 'close, foolish, even absurd' attention to that junk.

He began 'playing department store archaeologist', studying and mentally cataloguing the cornucopia of products he couldn't have dreamed up if he tried: cheeseburger-flavoured Pringles, for instance.

I now play some version of this game every time I'm at Walmart. I challenge myself as I cross the parking lot: What's the most absurd product I will see? The most poetic? The saddest? The one most revealing of twenty-first-century America? The funniest? Occasionally I think I should propose a collaboration to Bogost: We can start buying our 'finds' and fill a gallery with them.

Probably it's better to just leave the game as it is.

TRESPASS

Urban Exploration (UE) is a generic and self-explanatory term, but it doubles as a name for a more specific practise. It entails a particular focus on 'temporary, obsolete, abandoned or derelict spaces', as Bradley L. Garrett writes in his book on the subject, *Explore Everything: Place-Hacking the City.*

'Urban explorers trespass', he continues, 'into derelict industrial sites, closed hospitals, abandoned military installations, sewer and storm networks, transportation and utility systems, shuttered businesses, foreclosed estates, mines, construction sites, cranes, bridges and bunkers, among other places'.

This sounds dangerous, because it is. Climbing around sewer systems and abandoned buildings can entail not just the evasion of guards and cameras but actual physical risk. *Explore Everything* opens with Garrett (a researcher in the School of Geography and the Environment at the University of Oxford) in police custody. He concedes that the UE crowd enjoys the 'outlaw' image, 'masked up and sneaking about'.

But exploring abandoned places, he argues, responds to the modern city as 'a place where sensory overload and increased securitisation have become the norm, where the only acceptable modes of behaviour are to work and spend money on prepackaged "entertainment"'. He likes to call urban exploration *place-hacking*, a form of exploiting 'fractures in the architecture of the city' as a computer hacker exploits flaws in code.

This offers an alternative appreciation of history – history that is not being intentionally preserved and managed like an official heritage site but is instead deteriorating. Even the UE enthusiast's documentation of mundane-sounding but forbidden spaces like an abandoned hospital or a disused section of a metro system serves the purpose of, as one explorer put it, prodding others to 'understand how much they're missing every day'. Another explorer says the practise 'allows the curious-minded to discover a world of behind-the-scenes sights'.

Behind-the-scenes sights deserve to be taken seriously, even if you're not convinced by the romance of radical trespassing.

Abandoned spaces have a lot to tell us even if they are no longer meant to be seen. Huge swathes of the city are off-limits by design; forbidden territories, vast and tiny, are everywhere.

Look out for them or even their traces. Consider what you might be missing. Consider finding out.

EAT SOMEWHERE DUBIOUS

When we think about food writers and restaurant critics, we think of their haute cuisine expertise and their evaluations of fancy restaurants. But the best of this lot also have an appetite for oddball out-of-the-way places in obscure neighbourhoods.

Jonathan Gold, whose food writing for the *Los Angeles Times* won him a Pulitzer Prize, was the master of this. In a sense, his entire career was grounded in a systematic effort to pay attention to the uncelebrated.

When he was not long out of college, Gold decided he would eat at every single restaurant on Pico Boulevard, which runs from downtown Los Angeles all the way to Santa Monica. As he later explained, there was nothing obvious about this impossible odyssey. Other LA thorough-fares boasted more famous restaurants – or just better ones. 'But precisely because Pico is so unremarked, because it is left alone like old lawn furniture mouldering away in the side yard of a suburban house, it is at the centre of entry-level capitalism in central Los Angeles', Gold wrote. The street cuts through a dizzying variety of diverse neighbour-hoods, revealing multiple and overlapping visions of Los Angeles and its inhabitants. And that, he argued, made it 'one of the most vital food streets in the world'.

Yes, Gold freely admitted, he endured plenty of bad meals. But he also enjoyed and discovered outstanding food he'd never even heard of. And the exercise forced him to walk into and experience an endless variety of places he would not have been drawn to otherwise. 'It was the year I learned to eat', he later wrote. And it offered him a completely new perspective on his own city.

Mimic this feat on a smaller scale by reversing the way you typically decide where to eat, whether in your hometown or somewhere new. Instead of choosing the familiar chain, the internet-endorsed hot spot or the place that simply looks really interesting . . . choose the opposite.

That bland-looking eatery in some ugly shopping mall that has no Yelp reviews? Give it a try! Take in the atmosphere; ask questions about the menu; slyly observe the other patrons. Then take a few minutes to explore the nearby area. Maybe you'll get to brag to your friends about the delicious food you discovered. Either way, you'll experience a new place, for yourself.

READ THE PLAQUE

👁

Plaques and monuments are designed for your attention – and yet they remain widely neglected. Face it: You've likely walked right past many more public plaques than you've ever paused to read.

Roman Mars, creator of the popular podcast series *99% Invisible,* has made 'Read the Plaque' a recurring mantra. As he repeatedly points out, plaques often tell fascinating stories hidden in plain sight. The website readtheplaque.com offers thousands of examples on an interactive map – one plaque in New Zealand grumpily announces that it marks the spot of a forty-year-old tree that was 'felled by the bureaucracy . . . to make space for one more car'.

So if you spot one – and *especially* if it's placed next to something that looks completely unremarkable – try Mars's advice.

It hurts to be present.

MARIE HOWE

RECORD TEN METAPHOR-FREE OBSERVATIONS ABOUT THE ACTUAL WORLD THIS WEEK

Poet Marie Howe asks her students to write down 'ten observations of the actual world' every week. What she has in mind sounds fairly simple. 'Just tell me what you saw this morning, like in two lines. "I saw a water glass on a brown tablecloth, and the light came through it in three places"', she explained during an interview on the public radio show *On Being*. 'No metaphor. It's very hard'.

The tricky part, it turns out, is that 'no metaphor' bit. 'We want to say, 'It was *like* this; it was *like* that.' We want to look away', Howe continued. Somehow just noting and describing a glass of water is not enough. There is a sense that, to make our observation worthy of recording, we must elevate it to some more meaningful form. 'To resist metaphor is very difficult, because you have to actually endure the thing itself', she said. 'Which hurts us for some reason'.

Howe tells her students: no abstractions or interpretations. And after a few weeks, they get it. 'It is so thrilling', she said. 'I mean, it is thrilling. Everybody can feel it. Everyone is just like, "Wow." The slice of apple, and then that gleam of the knife, and the sound of the trash can closing, and the maple tree outside, and the blue jay. I mean, it almost comes clanking into the room. And it's just amazing'.

The students, she suggested, have finally worked around their need to *interpret* and have simply found a way to *engage* with the world as it is, through their senses – 'just noticing what's around them', without comparison, without reference point or metaphorical shortcut.

After five or six weeks, when the students have got this down, she tells them it's now okay to use metaphors. 'They're like, "Why would I? Why would I compare that to anything when it's itself?"' Howe concluded. 'Exactly. Good question'.

INVENT YOUR OWN RULES FOR SHARED SPACES

Signage usually instructs us in what *not* to do. 'No Parking'. 'Noise-Restricted Zone'. 'No Animals or Skateboards'. We take in these rules and directives on an almost unconscious level.

But consider taking such forms as a sort of challenge. In this case, what kind of restrictive zone would *you* create if you had the power?

As a means of discouraging street harassment, activist groups Feminist Apparel and Pussy Division once devised a series of dozens of 'No Catcall Zone' signs and installed them in city neighbourhoods. Their style mimicked official civic signage well enough to inspire a double take. Some of their signs were strictly text-based, using the colour and typography of 'No Parking' markers; others incorporated symbols (including, amusingly, a cat figure) in that shadow-person style that bureaucrats perfected long ago.

Look out for visual instructions laying out the rules and terms of the spaces you move through. Observe the behaviours happening around you and see where a little official (-looking) guidance might make this part of the world a better place.

ANNOTATE THE WORLD

The Wadsworth House, built in 1726 and now used for administrative offices, is one of the oldest buildings on Harvard University's campus. In the past it served as the home to a number of university presidents, whose names were later listed on a blocky grey monument just outside.

In 2015, someone added a pink sheet of paper to that monument, serving as a real-world annotation. It read: 'This house was also a place of enslavement. Among those held in bondage in this building were: Titus, Venus, Juba, Bilhah'. Titus, Venus, Juba and Bilhah were slaves owned by a couple of the Harvard presidents listed on the monument just above the pink sheet. This was the work of the 'Harvard and Slavery' project, spun out of a seminar at the school dedicated to exploring the neglected subject of slavery's role in the school's legacy.

'As debates about the institutional role of history divide campuses nationwide', the online publication *Atlas Obscura* reported at the time, 'annotating monuments has become one way for students to comment on their schools' commemorative choices without erasing them. Students at both the University of Missouri and William & Mary in Virginia have covered statues of Thomas Jefferson with sticky notes that detail some of his less heroic attributes'.

Whether as a form of protest or education or both, the real-world annotation offers a new filter for the world. What landmark or monument do you already know that tells a story of itself – but not the *whole* story? What would you add for others to learn? And as you encounter new landmarks and monuments, what questions can you ask to find out more that might currently be hidden or at least left out?

Less than a year after that original annotation was posted on the Wadsworth monument, Harvard added a permanent stone plaque to the building, memorialising the four slaves and making the annotation part of the official story.

COMPOSE A PERSONAL PLAQUE

Years ago, my friend Bob Safian wrote a moving piece for *The Ameri-can Lawyer,* where we both worked at the time, about the murder of his cousin. Their relationship was brotherly and the death was a devastating blow to Bob. At some point, he visited the physical scene of the crime and it struck him that there was nothing to mark its awful significance.

He speculated about an alternate reality in which every murder scene was clearly and lastingly marked – with a plaque, perhaps, to perman-ently commemorate what happened and who was lost.

The essay has stayed with me for a long time.

There's an echo of Bob's speculation in the long-running campaign of installing ghost bikes – bicycles painted white – as roadside memorials near intersections or other locations where cyclists have been killed by motorists. More recently, I was reminded again of this notion by the work of Philadelphia artist Lily Goodspeed.

Her project, which she calls 'Plaque to the Future', offers an 'unusual take on commemorative plaques', a post on the blog of podcast *99% Invis-ible* explained. 'Conventional metal plaques cost more money, need to meet notability requirements and feature deceased individuals'. Good-speed created 'waterproof stickers' resembling a traditional plaque and showed 'there is room to rethink those limiting criteria'.

These sticker 'plaques' document small moments of personal signifi-cance and workaday wonder.

'Derek B. was walking along Dickinson Street in July of 2017', one reads, 'when he saw a woman open her door, overhand throw a ⅔ eaten hot dog (still in the bun and topped with ketchup and pickles) into this tele-phone pole, and then close the door again. Derek has so many questions'.

Others document incidents such as a pug's running amok in a pharmacy or places like a park in which several friends had all experienced romantic breakups.

To this day, the memory of Bob's essay makes me wonder about the secret history of any given street corner. Goodspeed's project offers another way of thinking about the same idea, one that I consider when I revisit some familiar spot that has meaning to me and almost no one else: the park bench I paused on after learning I'd got a job, the awning we stood under when I said a final goodbye to someone, the stretch of country road where a careless bike accident broke my arm.

I don't need plaques to mark these places. But when I re-encounter them, I like to stop and think about what such a marker might say.

KEEP A NATURE LOG

Tom Weis is a designer who also teaches at the Rhode Island School of Design. In connection with a class about natural systems, which involved exploring and understanding local wetlands, he required students to spend one hour a week outside recording observations in nature. 'Similar to keeping a ship's log, I had them recording weather, tides (if near the water), foliage, temperature changes, etc.', he says.

Apply this idea to some specific patch of nature near you. Keep a nature log for the nearest park or community garden or empty lot, with the parameters adjusted according to the specifics of the land you're attending to. Review the data; present your observations to a neighbourhood group.

MAKE A ONE-MINUTE VIDEO ABOUT A PLACE

Paola Antonelli, the senior curator, department of architecture and design, at New York's Museum of Modern Art, is a highly original thinker, with a voracious curiosity guided by a distinctly forward-looking vision. When I asked her if she could suggest an exercise that would help the rest of us get better at noticing and attention, she started by contradicting the now-familiar advice that begins with putting down your devices. **'A phone', she argued, 'can trigger an obsessiveness that can lead to discoveries and truly deep learning'.**

Antonelli's visionary 2011 show *Talk to Me* included a project called 'myblocknyc', which encouraged individuals to create one-minute videos about their street and compile these on an interactive map, making it possible to explore the city through the sensibilities of locals.

With this in mind, Antonelli suggested: think of your phone as a kind of divining rod that might help you discover what's interesting and notable and worthy of a short video. Do this 'wherever you choose', she continued, 'your bedroom, your grandfather's farm, a dim sum restaurant, the subway'. You might jump from one designed object to another, constructing a kind of narrative. Decide how many you want to feature and why. Edit the video down to a single minute that depicts a place and the things defining it.

MAKE A FIELD GUIDE

Field guides – catalogues of birds or plants or elements of the natural world that are meant to serve as references and aids in the field – have been around since at least the nineteenth century. An artist and ornithologist named Roger Tory Peterson is often credited with devising what may now be the most familiar version of the form. Peterson's original collection of his colour illustrations of various birds was published in a 1930s guide book and proved to be an enduring franchise. My parents constantly toted an edition of the *Peterson Field Guide to Birds of North America*, one of many guides using the Peterson Identification System still in print.

The educational spirit of the field guide has since been carried over to address elements of the world created by humans. Designer Peter Dawson explicitly compares his book *The Field Guide to Typography: Typefaces in the Urban Landscape* to the sort of reference a bird watcher would carry. In a sense, Dawson's book is an overview of and introduction to typography. There are a lot of those already, but its conceptualisation as a field guide makes it a valuable reference that helps budding design geeks learn the names of type styles they encounter (or learn to look for) on signage and elsewhere in the world.

My favourite field guides are even more idiosyncratically specific. *The Container Guide,* published by Tim Hwang and Craig Cannon, is a meticulously researched guide to shipping containers. Ingrid Burrington's *Networks of New York: An Illustrated Field Guide to Urban Internet Infrastructure* teaches its readers the meaning of cryptic pavement markings that actually refer to the placement and specifications of cable and fibre-optic lines; the corporate connections to certain manhole covers; and the physical location of notable data centres and similar facilities of interest to anyone attempting to 'see the internet'.

Arguably the most famous unconventional field guide is Julian Montague's 2006 *The Stray Shopping Carts of Eastern North America: A Guide to Field Identification,* which offers a deadpan absurd and meticulously thought-out breakdown of the twenty-one varieties of 'true stray' shopping trolleys, and the nine 'false stray' varieties, carefully distinguishing, say, the 'plaza drift' varieties that have migrated only as far as another retail parking lot from the 'refuse receptacle' (which comes in two variations).

This combination of specificity and flexibility is where the field guide idea starts to get fun and potentially useful. Consider recurring sets of objects or personality types or almost anything in a particular setting you know, such as your neighbourhood or your office. How about a *Field Guide to Area Dogs*, based on your observations? Determine names, physical descriptions, relative friendliness and barking styles. Or research a *Field Guide to Intriguing Personal Objects Spotted in Cubicles on the Fourth Floor.* Come up with your own idea. Whether you produce such volumes is hardly the point. It's the fieldwork of noticing that you're after.

TEST YOURSELF

Look at something stationary, look away and then jot down everything you saw. Now look back and see how you did.

This thought comes from City College of New York sociology professor William Helmreich. And it reminds me of something furniture designer George Nelson once asked: 'Can you describe the colours and patterns of any rug in your dwelling? The wallpaper in the bedroom? The pictures in the front hall? When were they last looked at?'

Nelson tried the game himself. He guessed as to how many faces (animal or human; painted, printed, photographed, or carved) he would find in his own living room: about a dozen, he figured. Then he began to count. 'I scored very badly', he conceded. He'd expected about a dozen. He found around four hundred.

Test yourself.

4

CONNECTING
WITH OTHERS

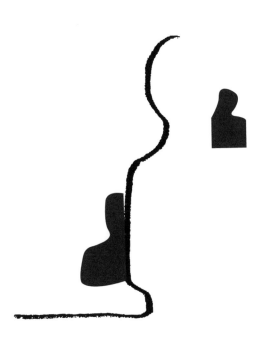

The quieter you become,

the more you can hear.

RAM DASS

CHANNEL YOUR INNER MONK

'Silence', reports a resident of Quebec's Oka Abbey, the oldest Trappist monastery in North America, 'is listening'.

Trappist monks are known for adhering to a vow of silence. This monk made his observations in writing, through an email exchange with a reporter. But in practise the residents of Oka Abbey *do* speak to one another sometimes – but only to 'convey necessary information' as they do the monastery's work. The key isn't not speaking at all – it's speaking only *when necessary*.

'We follow the Rule of St Benedict', this monk explained, 'and the first word of that rule is "Listen". That's the great ethical element of silence: to check my words and listen to another point of view'.

Another monk added: 'Is silence beneficial for all people? **I would say the cultivation of silence is indispensable to being human**. People sometimes talk as if they were "looking for silence", as if silence had gone away or they had misplaced it somewhere. But it is hardly something they could have misplaced. Silence is the infinite horizon against which is set every word they have ever spoken, and they can't find it? Not to worry – it will find them'.

Imagine following the spirit of a silence vow into daily life. Challenge yourself to spend an entire day saying only what you absolutely *must* say. It's been widely observed by behavioural psychology experts – and anyone who's ever been on a first date – that we too often tend to treat 'conversation' as a game of waiting for our own turn to speak. We miss what's being said because we're mentally rehearsing our next utterance.

What if you could eliminate the idea that the next available mini-silence is your next opening to express whatever is in your head? What if you were limited to, say, fifty spoken words tomorrow? I think you'd listen quite differently. You'd attend quite carefully to every word you heard. You'd be attuned to what you *must* respond to. You might discover that the less you say, the more you hear.

Silence isn't an endgame.

It's a catalyst,

an opportunity to discover

truer things about the world

outside or inside your head.

DIANE COOK

APPLY THE SLANT METHOD

You're not going to absorb the lessons of history or maths or literature if your jumpy mind can't focus on classroom lectures or discussions. Plenty of educators will tell you that jumpy minds are a pervasive problem, and some – including Barry Schwartz, a Swarthmore psychology professor and the author of *The Paradox of Choice* – argue for deliberate efforts to develop a 'sustained attention muscle' in students.

One specific approach used in some schools goes by the acronym SLANT: *s*it up; *l*ean forward; *a*sk and answer questions; *n*od your head and *t*rack the speaker.

This can be easily followed in any meeting or conversation.

Sitting up and leaning forward are self-explanatory. Asking questions both signals and fosters deeper engagement. Nodding displays understanding and enhances connection. To track the speaker simply means to look at the person speaking, which in addition to baseline civility also means students find it easier to process what they are hearing.

A teacher can use the SLANT strategy as a prod to students to behave in a manner that builds the 'attention muscle', as Schwartz put it in a column for *Slate*. It also offers all of us a handy mental checklist to enforce on ourselves. Run through it the next time you realise you're in a conversation that deserves more engagement than you're giving it.

LISTEN SELFLESSLY

We all know what it feels like to be in effect *forced* to listen – and why sometimes even the best of us just can't put up with that.

But sometimes we can and should. The best advice I've ever encountered about practising selfless listening came from *Wall Street Journal* relationship-advice columnist Elizabeth Bernstein, quoting one of her readers. The reader was a sixty-six-year-old accountant who 'believes there is no greater gift than genuinely listening to a person, without interrupting or judging or inserting your opinion'.

And his facilitative tactic? Breathing.

When he listens – and particularly when what he's hearing makes him feel defensive or want to react – he starts taking deep breaths. He attributes this idea to some kind of Marine sniper training, but it's actually pretty straightforward stuff, an ancient practise now backed by modern science. Deep breaths dampen the production of cortisol, a hormone produced by the adrenal glands in stressful moments.

'That breath stops time', he asserts – sharpens his hearing, dials him into nonverbal cues, opens him up emotionally. 'It gives you a space and it gives the other person a space'. In a relationship, of course, that's crucial. But it can come in handy in almost any interaction.

There's no reason to learn how to *show* you're

paying attention, if you are in fact paying attention.

CELESTE HEADLEE

TALK TO A STRANGER

I'm a naturally shy person, so it never occurred to me that strangers could provide attention inspiration until a couple of my students suggested it.

Writer and teacher Kio Stark makes a nice case for talking to strangers in her book *When Strangers Meet: How People You Don't Know Can Transform You*. She offers encouraging tips for people who might not take to this sort of thing naturally.

And that's not just me. Particularly in shared public spaces, most of us observe what sociologists call *civil inattention*, silently agreeing not to bother one another in a kind of mutual noninterference pact. Stark advocates finding small opportunities to violate these mores – just a little.

If you see someone who looks like he or she might need, for example, directions, resist the urge to dart past, eyes averted. Offer to help. One of my students did something like this. When an elderly woman directed a random comment at him about rubbish that littered the street, he engaged, listened, responded. The encounter was fleeting, but it made an impression on him.

When you feel comfortable being open to such moments, Stark advises, create them yourself. Ask a question; offer compliments; try 'tossing out casual observations about the shared space you're inhabiting'.

Stark offers the commonsense caveats you'd expect: don't bother someone who looks hurried, don't confuse 'giving compliments' with harassment, don't be rude, etc.

But be open. As Stark advises, the important thing is to ask a question and then be quiet: **'Give people a chance to fill their own silences'.** That is actually an old trick known to interviewers and reporters – we all have an instinct to break up an awkward pause, but it's better to resist and let the other person do it. 'Once someone feels listened to', Stark writes, 'they can't stop talking'.

Then again, maybe the connection doesn't have to be verbal. The sweetest example I've encountered involves an anecdote Stark shares about one of her students – poetically suggesting how we might talk to a stranger without saying a thing. The student was on the underground, listening to music through headphones, seated next to a woman doing the same thing. 'He took off his headphones and held them out to her', Stark writes. 'She looked puzzled for a moment, then took hers off and traded with him'. After a few minutes, they switched back. 'Not a word passed between them'.

SEEK OUT STRANGERS

Radio producer Aaron Henkin took a very structured approach to engaging with strangers. His goal: 'to meet and interview everybody who lived and worked on one city block in Baltimore'. The result was an audio documentary – and a lot of lessons learned from talking to people he didn't know.

Imagine adopting this tactic to meet and talk to everyone on *your* street or in your office or at the place you swim on the weekends or whatever. You don't have to produce anything, of course. Connecting with these strangers (even the ones who are sort of familiar to you) will be payoff enough.

GAMIFY A STRANGER

Suppose you are as shy as I am and can't always bring yourself to talk to people you don't know. This does not mean you must pretend that no one else exists. Perhaps, without anyone being the wiser, you can make a stranger your muse.

There are plenty of examples of photographers and other artists documenting strangers. But I like what artists Daniel Koren and Vania Heymann came up with. Koren noticed that he was uncomfortable walking in sync with random fellow pedestrians – until he started to think of the experience as a race (a race that only he was aware of). Koren and Heymann ended up making a hilarious video called *Walking Contest*, converting this everyday instance of discomfort into a highly relatable comment on the nature of human interaction.

The reward here is the value of paying creative attention to strangers. You really never know what they'll do and there are endless ways to engage with them – even if the interaction plays out only in your own mind.

LET A STRANGER LEAD YOU

Artist Vito Acconci's notorious *Following Piece* was performed over a period of weeks in 1969. Daily he would choose a person at random and follow her or him around New York. This would continue until his subject (who had no idea this was happening) entered a space Acconci could not – a residence, for instance, or a car that promptly sped away. The exercise could last a few minutes or hours, depending on what the stranger happened to do. In one case, Acconci sat through a movie when his target went to the cinema.

Acconci didn't see his efforts as either exercises in courting danger or voyeurism, or even, particularly, curiosity about his subjects. 'It was sort of a way to get myself off the writer's desk and into the city', he said years afterward. **'It was like I was praying for people to take me somewhere I didn't know how to go myself'.**

In the 1980s, artist Sophie Calle also took to following strangers and on one occasion was subsequently introduced to one of her targets at a party. He mentioned he would soon be taking a trip to Venice – and she decided to follow him there. She travelled to the city and took several days to find him, whereupon she began to track him as best she could – until eventually he recognised her. This became the subject of her book *Suite Vénitienne,* which concerns itself with matters of surveillance and stalking, but whose discoveries also include, as one critic put it, the basic truth that 'we move through the days on our own internal missions, mysterious and unknowable to anyone outside'.

Borrowing this sort of practise might require some nerve or entail some risk. But it could be a genuine adventure in seeing the new and unexpected. The game Pokémon Go was widely and specifically praised for the way it encouraged players to visit new places – and some rather mindlessly ended up at the edges of cliffs, in sketchy back alleys and in a number of vehicular accidents while pursuing their virtual prey. So perhaps the risk is relative.

PASS AN IDEOLOGICAL TURING TEST

Suppose you are concerned that your view of the world is too narrow and self-reinforcing – that you are stuck in a so-called filter bubble that leaves you most exposed to ideas and perspectives that you already agree with. As a result, you view opposing perspectives as not just wrong but, basically, crazy.

You deserve credit for even worrying about this. A prominent symptom of the widespread malady described is total denial of the possibility that other points of view might have some overlooked merit.

Tyler Cowen, a popular blogger and economics professor at George Mason University, is remarkable for his ability to deliver supremely confident judgements about everything from high-level policy issues to Texas barbecue. But even *he* has confessed to concern about living in a filter bubble. And he has offered some potential solutions.

'It's much harder to dislike people face-to-face than over the internet', he observes. 'You could insert yourself into an environment where you are a minority, and thus will feel an instinctive need to ingratiate yourself with others. So if you're a conservative, spend some time with academics in the humanities. If you're a progressive, visit a right-leaning church group'.

Cowen may be correct that this kind of face-to-face interaction is the most powerful strategy for addressing the filter bubble problem. It's also fairly difficult, involving time and resources you may not have.

So he makes a second suggestion – which he teasingly warns may be 'less pleasant, perhaps precisely because it may turn out to be effective'. Specifically, it means passing an 'ideological Turing test' (a phrase he attributes to his colleague Bryan Caplan). The original Turing test involved the attempt to devise a robot or computerised artificial intelligence that could 'pass' for a human. This iteration involves passing for a proponent of views you oppose.

'Keep a diary, write a blog, or set up a separate and anonymous Twitter account', he advises. 'And through that medium, write occasional material in support of views you don't agree with. Try to make them sound as persuasive as possible'. He offers the aside that if you need to 'keep your own sense of internal balance', you could make this take the form of a kind of opposing-views dialogue; and if you don't want to do this in public, create your entries offline and destroy them when you're done. But one way or another, spend time making 'the best case for the opposing point of view at least once a month'.

This brings us to the ideological Turing test. Can your articulation of a view you don't agree with pass muster with people who actually endorse it? Show your work to someone whose point of view you oppose and find out.

Inviting a loved one, a friend, or even a stranger

to record a meaningful interview with you just

might turn out to be one of the most important

moments in that person's life – and in yours.

DAVE ISAY

INTERVIEW A FRIEND, LOVED ONE, STRANGER – OR EVEN AN IDEOLOGICAL NEMESIS

Founded in 2003, StoryCorps facilitates conversations between self-selecting pairs of individuals – two friends, a mother and son, a romantic couple. These are performed as interviews often recorded at special StoryCorps booth facilities and archived with the American Folklife Center at the Library of Congress. Some end up being broadcast on National Public Radio; you may have heard a few. More than a hundred thousand people have participated.

A StoryCorps interview – indeed, the whole intellectual construct of an interview – inspires better listening because it changes the stakes. As founder Dave Isay has maintained (and as every journalist knows), the interview structure, maybe involving a microphone or a recorder or even just a pad and pen, gives the inquisitor licence to push beyond usual trivialities.

Isay learned by way of his work as a radio journalist that this is often more significant for the interviewee. 'The simple act of being interviewed could mean so much to people', he later related. 'Particularly those who'd been told that their stories didn't matter'. When he presented one of his subjects with a document of their conversations in the form of a book, the man's reaction involved literally shouting: 'I exist!' (This incident, in fact, was part of what led Isay to create StoryCorps.)

But can the interview construct help inspire better conversation and more effective listening and deepen connections? That really depends on asking good questions, which can be harder than it sounds. Celeste Headlee, a public radio host in Georgia, has offered a set of rules, drawn from her years of interviewing, for having 'a better conversation'.

Ask open-ended questions, not something that can be answered with a simple yes or no. You want the basic who, what, when, where, why and how facts, but you want to follow up to get *beyond* the facts. What was that like, how did that feel? If in conversation you are told something you don't understand, then say so; don't bullshit.

StoryCorps has published an amazing list of hundreds of potential questions, broken into multiple categories. While they are listed in no particular order, here are the first eleven. Start with these:

- Who has been the most important person in your life? Can you tell me about him or her?

- What was the happiest moment of your life? The saddest?

- Who has been the biggest influence on your life? What lessons did that person teach you?

- Who has been the kindest to you in your life? What are the most important lessons you've learned in life?

- What is your earliest memory?

- What is your favourite memory of me?

- Are there any funny stories your family tells about you that come to mind?

- Are there any funny stories or memories or characters from your life that you want to tell me about?

- What are you proudest of?

- When in life have you felt most alone?

'It takes some courage to have these conversations', Isay says. StoryCorps encourages participants to speak more or less directly to the mortality of the participants: We are doing this because we are all going to die and we want some things about us to persist. This is why Story-Corps interviews that end up on the radio often have the big impact they do: 'You're hearing something that's authentic and pure'.

The latest StoryCorps initiative might take even more courage to emulate. Its 'One Small Step' project encourages interviews between individuals with opposing political views. It's a bold idea – and one that just underscores how important it is to remember that truly listening takes real effort.

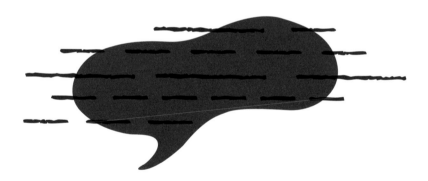

INTERVIEW AN ELDER

Gerontologist Karl Pillemer was already a recognised expert on ageing and the policies and programmes that aim to improve that universal process when he faced a mid-career dilemma. He wanted to close the gap between his abstract policy knowledge and the people it meant to serve. Then he had an epiphany. 'Why not', he wrote, 'begin with an activity as old as the human race: asking the advice of the oldest people you know? Because older people have one thing that the rest of us do not: they have lived their lives. They have been where we haven't. Indeed, people who have experienced most of a long life are in an ideal position to assess what "works" and what doesn't for finding a direction . . . They bring to our contemporary problems and choices perspectives from a different time'.

Pillemer suggests talking to some variation of your future self – a 'maven' of sorts who has lived a life and led a career that you admire or aspire to, who *embodies the "self" you would like to be*'. This person, he adds rather bluntly, 'should be old – and preferably *really* old. You don't want a forty-year-old if you are twenty; you want someone in his or her eighties or nineties, or a centenarian if you can find one'.

Who is the oldest person you know?

Who is the oldest person in your neighbourhood?

What could you ask them about that they might enjoy sharing?

There may be some trial and error here and maybe your first pass could be inspired by something you'd specifically like to know or learn about. But try to keep it open-ended enough so that you are both engaged.

Seeking advice – about anything at all – may not be a bad place to start when you are faced with a dilemma you're not sure how to solve. You could ask about a job your interviewees had early on or what they liked or didn't like about school or the first time they left home or the biggest risk they ever took or even what technologies made a difference or an impression in the past, from the interviewee's perspective.

What do they remember? What do they wish someone would ask?

IDENTIFY THE WEIRDEST THING IN THE ROOM AND ASK ABOUT IT

For a book called *Taking Things Seriously,* editors Joshua Glenn and Carol Hayes asked dozens of authors and designers to write short essays about an unusual object of personal significance to them, but one that would not be obviously significant to anybody else. In other words, not the latest luxury-design totem or cutting-edge gizmo, but the weird thing that occupies a surprising place of pride on the sitting room mantlepiece or an office desk.

Thus we learn that the odd foam construction that one designer displays is actually the packaging for a Grammy Award.

Novelist Lydia Millet keeps a ridiculous plastic dog figurine because of its unlikely association with a passionate romance.

A comically huge trophy turns out to be a gesture of apology awarded by a guilty boyfriend who missed a birthday party.

Cartoonist Bill Griffith has kept a decades-old empty bottle of an obscure soda called Zippy that he found on the street – because it inspired the logo for his popular comic strip.

There's a lesson in this. Whether you are in someone's home, office or business, determine which is the most inexplicable and unlikely object you can see. Then ask, 'So what's the story with that?' Chances are, a memorable tale will follow.

> Appreciate the random participation
>
> of others in our lives.

POETICISE THE IRRITATING

One of my favourite things to do', Kenneth Goldsmith announced in his book *Uncreative Writing*, 'is to walk a few steps behind two people engaged in conversation for several blocks'.

That sounds supremely annoying. But the often-counterintuitive Goldsmith (whose thoughts on Duchamp's 'infrathin' idea I referred to earlier) is taking a cue from John Cage's contention that music is everywhere if you just learn to listen for it. 'Poetry is all around us', Goldsmith writes – and that includes the poetry of two strangers blabbing, their conversation 'punctuated by red lights, giving the speech a certain pace and rhythm'.

The same applies, he argues, to the many mobile phone talkers who contribute noise to pavements and public spaces everywhere. Psychological research indicates that an overheard mobile phone call is actually more distracting than an overheard face-to-face conversation, partly because the unwilling listener's brain becomes engaged in trying to 'fill in the blanks' to make sense of what's come to be called a halfalogue. As one researcher explained: 'If you only hear one person speaking, you're constantly trying to place that part of the conversation in context'.

But Goldsmith argues that this, too, can be converted to poetry of a sort. 'I like to think of [their chatter] as a release', he writes, 'a new level of contextual richness, a reimagining of public discourse, half conversations resulting in a breakdown of narrative, a city full of people spewing remarkable soliloquies'.

The same idea can be applied to the visual.

Goldsmith and writer David Wondrich once explicitly looked for and documented minor flaws in the urban landscape – a 'semi-truncated ornament' outside a church, a missing screw on a sign next to an expensive building, a 'misaligned column-half' in front of a prominent hotel – and presented their findings in a poetic slide show titled 'Broken New York'.

IMAGINE WHAT SOMEONE IS THINKING

In her book *Bored and Brilliant,* radio host Manoush Zomorodi observes that on some level, the smartphone serves for many as a simple means of escape. She issued a series of challenges to her listeners to prod them back into the physical world.

One of the final challenges – 'observe something else' – urges readers to go somewhere ('a park, a mall, a petrol station, a café'), sit awhile, and just look. 'Pause and imagine what a single person is thinking', she suggests.

As easy as it sounds, this could be a nuanced exercise. You must choose your subject. You must do so based on observations that consider your subject's place in the world. You must invent a mood and a mind-set, based only upon what you can observe. You must imagine the arc of a story and where in that arc this person is right now.

You must devise a story whose ending you'll never know, even though you are the one telling it.

DONATE TIME

Maybe you feel pressed for time. There's too much to do, no opportunity to relax, concentrate or pause to appreciate the world. This sense of a personal *time famine* is not uncommon. To address this condition, one group of management scholars proposed a surprising remedy: **give some time away.**

Researchers divided their subjects into two groups. One group received a gift – they were directed to spend time on themselves and in some cases granted an unexpected time bonus by being let out of the study early. The other group was directed to spend an equal amount of time on someone else: cooking a special meal, writing a letter, helping a neighbour with some task, collecting litter in the park. Afterwards, members of each group were asked how whatever they'd done 'impacted their feelings of time famine'. The result, according to the researchers: 'those who spent time on others reported feeling like they had more time than those who spent time on themselves'.

Why would this be?

The scholars hypothesised that a time donation increases a sense of *self-efficacy*, defined as 'that (rare) feeling of being able to accomplish all that we set out to do'. Crossing an item off your personal to-do list may not have that same payoff, because it also reminds you of the *rest* of your to-do list.

But helping your neighbour clear out his garage is a self-contained accomplishment – something you *got done* that had 'a specific, tangible impact'.

What time donation could you make? Explore this a little: who could use some of your time and for what? Think about people you know, but also think beyond that. Ask others for ideas. Consider the possibilities you turn up. Pay attention to them. Then act.

ASK FIVE QUESTIONS. GIVE FIVE COMPLIMENTS

In a column for *The Wall Street Journal*, Alison Wood Brooks, an assistant professor in Harvard Business School's Negotiation, Organizations and Markets Unit, addressed the seemingly petty subject of improving workplace conversations. She included a couple of straightforward suggestions, one of which was to ask more questions and give more compliments.

According to the article, many typical (and forgettable) office chats involve simple exchanges of statements, which can be made more useful and memorable with the addition of a question or two. For instance, if someone says 'Nice presentation', don't just say thanks, but also add something like 'Anything you think I could improve on?' You might get some useful information – and you're signalling that you're open to more genuine engagement.

It's obvious enough why doling out compliments might improve personal interactions – but the trick lies in how you do it. An accidentally backhanded compliment ('You did really well for someone so new') can be more alienating than no compliment at all. So avoid qualifiers and try to be specific: 'Your presentation was really organised and efficient'.

These strategies can be used to ends well beyond office decorum or career advancement through small talk. They're helpful pointers for engaging with strangers, friends and all humans in between.

So in the course of a week, try to ask five questions and dole out five compliments. The questions don't need to be grandiose or existential, just honest expressions of curiosity. You'll find that this requires an alert attentiveness towards other people and what they're saying.

Complimenting others will have the same effect. Be thoughtful about this, of course: A man complimenting a woman on her skirt can be more creepy or threatening than engaging. But make an effort to notice things (including behaviours and actions) that might normally slip by unremarked.

If you're really in doubt – or just painfully shy – you might opt to note silently the things around you that *deserve* a compliment; it's a bit of a cop-out, but harmless. And it still has some payoff: the best way to seem more engaged is to *be* more engaged.

FIND SOMETHING TO COMPLAIN ABOUT

Complaining gets a bad rap. Of course it can be dangerous to simply *wallow* in the negative. But let's face it: without complaining, there can be no progress. The trick is to treat negativity as a means, not an end. James Murphy, the founder of LCD Soundsystem, has been credited with a nice aphorism:

'The best way to complain is to make things'.

He did not actually say that, but he once expressed something fairly close to its spirit. Instead of lamenting the fact that no one was making the music he wanted to hear, he set out to make that music himself.

In a very similar spirit, Seth Godin, the author and speaker, suggests one positively negative way to go about looking at the world: ask 'What's broken?'

What he means is: what, among everything you encounter, could be made better somehow? 'This exercise works for showers, trouser fasteners, checkout lines, gender roles and more', he says. He offers examples from his own observations: the taxi queue at the airport, inadequate concession staff at a cinema, an anti-crime sign riddled with bullets. The litany has a point: 'All around us is this huge potential – hidden potential – to make things unbroken'.

The subjectivity in these statements is important. Don't worry about whether someone else could counter that whatever you're complaining about is actually just fine the way it is. Negativity is *personal*. 'If I think it's broken, it's broken', Godin declares. 'You get to say the same thing!'

So look for the ugliest building (or car or jumper) of the day, the worst thing, the most broken thing, the thing that's so bad it makes you cross. That which angers or irritates or annoys you need not conquer you. It may amuse you or inspire you.

That which bothers you might just make your day.

COMPARE MEMORIES

'My real interest is in memory. I have a good one', artist Amanda Tiller once remarked, 'but unfortunately it's not for useful things'.

Tiller explores this theme over a diverse series of works that chronicle what she is able to recall, without consulting Google. The piece 'Movie Poster Prints' begins with her writing out her memory of a film's plot and converting those words into images. Her series of 'Genograms' involves embroidered flowcharts illustrating, for instance, all the connections she can make to *The Cosby Show* or *The Wonder Years*. The remarkable 'Everything That I Know' is a written documentation of exactly what the title suggests, all from memory, in an ongoing series of books.

'Through my work', Tiller states, 'I present my own knowledge, primarily recalled from memory, and invite the viewer to "compare notes"'. Comparing notes is key. Think about a trip you took at least ten years ago, ideally with someone else. Spend an hour trying to remember everything about it that you can.

Do not consult photographs or diary entries; just *remember*. In particular, try to remember the odd, small moments – not just the spectacular cathedral, but the young man you glimpsed in the hotel lobby. Concentrate on what lingers in your memory, however apparently inconsequential. Write down everything you can recall.

Discuss your findings with your travelling partner from that journey and see what lines up and what doesn't – and what that person recalls. Consider the difference between immediate experience and what sticks in your mind later. Consider how this affects what you choose to try to remember right now.

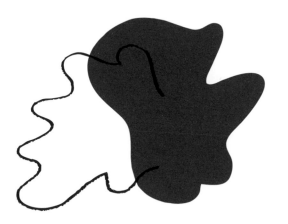

WRITE A LETTER

One thing I realise I love about the 'letter' as a form is that it's conversation – always available. You can just sit down any old morning & have a conversation whether the person's there or not. You can talk about anything & you don't have to wait politely for the other person to finish the train of thought. You can have long gaps between passages – days can go by & you might return & pick it up again. And the great difference in all other forms of writing is that it is dependent to a large extent on the other person. It's not just a solo act. You're writing in response to or in relationship to someone else – over time. I think that's the key – over time.

That is Sam Shepard, in a letter to his 'dearest friend' Johnny Dark, as quoted by brainpickings.org creator Maria Popova. (A selection of Shepard and Dark's correspondence, drawn from letters that are part of The Wittliff Collections, has been gathered in the 2013 book *Two Prospectors*.)

Popova is a great advocate of the traditional letter as a form. Separately, in fact, Popova has excavated a Lewis Carroll pamphlet titled *Eight or Nine Wise Words About Letter-Writing* and some of his rules are *more* useful in the digital age. For instance: if you find yourself making a hot reply to something annoying, put your message aside for a day and reread it as though it was written to you.

If you're answering a correspondent who has made 'a severe remark', Carroll wrote, 'either leave it unnoticed, or make your reply distinctly *less* severe: and if he makes a friendly remark, tending towards "making up" the little difference that has arisen between you, let your reply be

> The very thing that makes the epistolary art so singularly powerful [is] its ability to transport the recipient to the sender's world and welcome one consciousness into the felt experience of another.
>
> MARIA POPOVA

distinctly *more* friendly'. And on a related note, Carroll advised: Don't try to get in the last word.

Whether you're writing to an old pal or a current antagonist, the letter *can* be a medium that rewards thoughtfulness and care.

Write to a friend you've been out of touch with. Write to an enemy you're ready to stop fighting with. Devote real time and attention to the enterprise. Consider what you want to say and be open to the idea that it may take two or three tries to say it right.

Write to:

A HERO

A VILLAIN

A LOVER

YOUR PARENTS

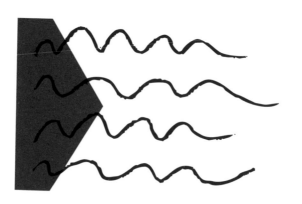

WRITE A LETTER TO A STRANGER

Not long out of college, and struggling with depression, Hannah Brencher found solace in the written word. Brencher's mother did not like to use email and Brencher came to deeply appreciate her handwritten letters. 'I did the only thing I could think of at the time', she said later, recounting that trying period. 'I wrote those same kinds of letters that my mother had written me, for strangers, and tucked them all throughout the city, dozens and dozens of them. I left them everywhere, in cafés and in libraries, at the UN, everywhere'.

This curious project became a minor sensation. Her blog about the practise caught on and she offered to write a letter to anybody who wanted one, for whatever reason. Eventually this led to a book and morphed into a new enterprise called The World Needs More Love Letters (MoreLoveLetters.com), through which requests for letters are channelled to willing letter writers, resulting in hundreds of 'love letter bundles' crisscrossing the country.

This is a deeply charming notion, which with a little tweaking inspires a fresh approach to the consideration of others. Spend some time as you move through the world thinking about the strangers you encounter. To whom might you write a letter and what might you say? 'Stranger' can include people you've encountered regularly without really knowing: a certain friendly cashier, a memorable waiter, a security person at your bank.

Actually delivering the letter isn't important. (Although, when I recall certain strangers in places I used to live, I wish I'd written them a letter of goodbye.) But writing it *is* important.

The online magazine *The Awl* used to run a terrific occasional series called 'Stranger of the Week', written in the form of a letter to someone who will (most likely) never see it, appreciating and wondering about this individual who, in a brief crossing of paths, made an impression.

A stranger on the underground hauling a box marked 'Kerri's Memories' becomes the starting point for an artful speculation about its contents and what story they might tell. A pavement encounter with a man carrying flowers sparks a meditation on the vagaries of intra-gender small talk.

Be alert to the stranger who might accidentally inspire you.

When you talk to strangers, you make beautiful and

surprising interruptions in the expected narrative of

your daily life. You shift perspective.

KIO STARK

MEET A FRIEND HALFWAY

Artist Christopher Robbins is an *auto interventionist* – a term he uses to describe the practise of 'intervening in your own life'. His first meeting with another artist, Douglas Paulson, makes for a good example. Robbins wrote to Paulson with the hope that the two might collaborate. At the time, he was living in Copenhagen and Paulson was in Serbia. Paulson was amenable and suggested they meet 'halfway'.

Robbins later explained: 'I thought I was being a smartass by saying, "Oh, yeah, halfway?" I looked at Google Earth and said, "Here's the exact halfway point, is this what you meant?" And he was like, "Yeah, exactly, that's what I meant"'.

They arranged to meet at a lake in the Czech Republic – the precise geographic midpoint between them.

Later, Robbins and Paulson converted this experience into an exercise for the first episode of the PBS Digital Studios production *The Art Assignment*. 'Pick a friend, and calculate the exact geographic midpoint between where the two of you live', the Robbins and Paulson assignment begins. Sites such as www.geomidpoint.com or of course a paper map, can help. Having picked a place, decide on a date and time to meet.

It turns out that meeting halfway is an idea with some notable artistic precedents. In 1988, Marina Abramović and Ulay walked from opposite directions to meet at the midpoint of the Great Wall of China, to mark the end of their romantic relationship and professional collaboration.

In 1999, Francis Alÿs and a collaborator arrived separately in Venice. Each wandered around carrying half of a tuba until they finally ran into each other – at which point they assembled the tuba and played a single note.

Such projects force participants to deal with the physical environment in a particular way, imposing meaning on an arbitrary space. As the *Art Assignment* host Sarah Urist Green observed, it also spoke to personal relationships: **'Who do you trust to hold the other half of your tuba?'**

With that in mind, you can modify this gesture for a variety of situations. A reunion convergence from great distances might be particularly thrilling, but try using this method to settle on a lunch spot with a local friend. Maybe the midpoint is close to some restaurant you've never heard of or, even better, some unfamiliar public place.

For Paulson and Robbins's first meeting, one agreed to bring food, the other drinks. Perhaps you could each choose to walk to the destination and share with each other pictures taken along the way. A routine lunch becomes a singular journey. That's what a self-intervention is all about.

DESCRIBE THE NIGHT SKY

Few of us know our night skies intimately. In an essay for *Aeon* about our knowledge of the stars in the sky, scholar Gene Tracy shared a brief but lovely anecdote. It concerned a man who, upon arriving at some night-time destination, had the habit of calling his wife to let her know where he was – and to describe the stars. 'She scanned the sky at her end', Tracy wrote. 'In that way, he connected with her, both of them finding one another in the world through that useful intelligence of distant stars'.

This could work from across town or across the country. You'll have to look up and look carefully, and both describe and listen with patience and precision. But as far apart as you might be, the night sky can connect you.

WALK AND TALK

'Instead of suggesting a coffee or lunch meeting', writer and entrepreneur Sarah Kathleen Peck advises, 'suggest a walking meeting'. To back this up, she's worked out a whole considered structure. Peck's walking meetings are intended to last two and a half hours, with the first thirty or so minutes reserved for a gradual gathering and introductions. Participants then walk for an hour and a half.

'Watch for the natural rhythms of conversation and walking: people tend to walk for twenty minutes, and then pause, which is true for conversations as well. Let this happen naturally', she writes on her site sarahkpeck.com. Larger groups will tend to spread out, with different participants moving at different paces. If the route is complicated, provide a map; if not, just agree on an end point. 'In my groups of twelve, people will separate into pairs or groups of three to four to talk about ideas. Let the accordion of walkers expand, and then contract over time and space'.

She often wraps it up with a final half hour of 'regrouping' at the end, perhaps involving a reflection or a question or two. Do this once a month, Peck suggests; gather feedback and let the practise evolve. The walk can be overtly focused on the environment (noises, sights, physical sensations), on some other topic agreed upon in advance or on nothing at all. Doing this even once with one friend has great appeal as an alternative to the usual chat over coffee or drinks – a novel pairing of conversation and movement.

CONSTRUCT A COLLECTIVE BIOGRAPHY

In her book *Textbook Amy Krouse Rosenthal,* Krouse Rosenthal offered up what she called 'The Short, Collective Biography Experiment', which she devised in collaboration with artist Lenka Clayton.

First, gather a group of people, perhaps over dinner. The specific nature of the group doesn't actually matter that much – friends, colleagues, acquaintances or some combination of those categories. 'Through conversation', Krouse Rosenthal writes, 'endeavour to find a collection of autobiographical statements that are equally true for each and every member of the group'. Throw out questions: are we all from America? Do we all like flannel? This might last thirty minutes or go on for hours. 'You'll know when to wrap it up'.

At that point: 'Assemble your statements. Call it your Short, Collective Biography'.

This strikes me as a brilliant way of getting to know others, both familiar and unfamiliar. It deserves to be a craze.

WALK TOGETHER SILENTLY

'A friend of mine', writes Rob Forbes, the founder of Design Within Reach, 'leads groups on hour-long nature walks', with an important catch: no talking. 'Only at the end of the hike do they discuss what they experienced, with the idea being that silence allows our senses to take over, so we can smell, see and hear more accurately. This exercise is designed to keep your mind alert to what is really around you in the moment'.

The responsibility to notice is quietly pushed back onto each individual. You can't rely on the guide to point out important details or your peer to catch the interesting side attractions. And you don't want to be the one person in the after-discussion who missed all the cool stuff along the way. In fact, you want to be the one who picked up on something unique.

Maybe this sounds like a good way to ruin a walk with a completely unnecessary layer of de facto competition. But it could also be fun and maybe the game-like element could be playfully amplified. Best noticer gets a free drink at the after-walk discussion?

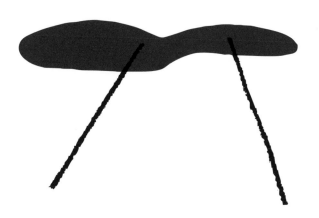

5

BEING ALONE

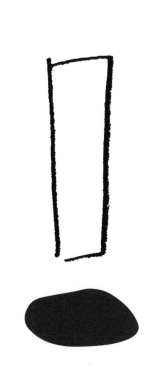

> We don't devote as much attention to any one thing, and we sacrifice the quality of our attention. When we are mindful, some of that attentional flightiness disappears as if of its own accord.
>
> MARIA KONNIKOVA

UNITASK

I grew up in a rural part of Texas, where my absolute least favourite chore was mowing our big tree-sparse garden – particularly in the summer. I hated it and vowed to live a lawn-free life. Today my all-time favourite non-possession is a lawn mower.

So it was with some fascination that I read blogger Jason Kottke's confession that he finds mowing the lawn 'extremely satisfying'. He claimed he could achieve both 'euphoric giddiness' and a 'simultaneously calming' feeling from 'making all the grass the same height, surrounding the remaining uncut lawn with concentric rectangles of freshly mowed grass'. He also praised the virtues of bagging shopping at the supermarket: 'Getting all those different types of products – with their various shapes, sizes, weights, levels of fragility, temperatures – quickly into the least possible number of bags . . . quite pleasurable. Reminds me a little of Tetris'.

It sounds weird, but this is actually called *unitasking* or *monotasking* – a wilfully one-thing-at-a-time antidote to the endlessly hyped notion of multitasking. Or, as one writer noted, 'a twenty-first-century term for what your high school English teacher probably just called "paying attention"'.

Unitasking can involve devoting your undivided attention to a single conversation or to reading a novel, but it's most intriguing when applied to something that has no intrinsic appeal at all.

There's nothing wrong with watching Netflix while folding clothes or enjoying a podcast while cleaning the sink. But game designer and philosopher Ian Bogost (whose thinking I cited in the item about turning a visit to a department store into a game) makes a case for giving mundane tasks like cleaning and folding laundry your full attention, rather than distracting yourself with simultaneous entertainment. Specifically, he makes the case for . . . mowing the lawn.

'It's an example I love because it's the kind of thing that no one would intuitively call a fun experience', he told an interviewer. 'But then when you do it, you discover something you haven't seen before . . . It's almost like, **the more you're drowning in familiarity, the better the fun is.** It requires less novelty to produce even more gratification'.

The key here, in Bogost's thinking, is recognising that the something you may discover doesn't come from you, but from your openness to whatever you're unitaskingly doing. 'It wasn't you who had to come up with that meaning', Bogost said. 'It was given to you by the world. And once you get yourself on that path where you're willing to find something delightful in laundry and in dishwashers, it means that you train yourself to be able to find it almost anywhere in almost anything'.

So go and mow the lawn.

BE ALONE IN PUBLIC

To some people, eating alone feels like the scene from the 1984 movie *The Lonely Guy* in which the character played by Steve Martin requests a table for one. A giant spotlight is triggered and patrons fall silent to follow his journey through the crowded room to his solo table.

Educator Andrew Reiner described in a *New York Times* essay how he asks students to get over this fear, with a particularly draconian assignment. 'Eat in a crowded university dining room', he commands, 'without the company of schoolwork, laptops or smartphones. Or friends'. There's something to be said for trying this out.

Reiner is teaching intimacy, connection and vulnerability – particularly in the social networking era. Many students are unnerved by this assignment, feeling judged and self-conscious.

But one interesting study challenges our underlying fears of being alone and judged. Researchers intercepted and nudged college students to make a quick visit to an art gallery, either alone or in a group. Subjects were asked to gauge how much they figured they would enjoy the experience. Those who had to go it alone were notably more pessimistic about the prospect.

But they needn't have been. 'There was no statistically significant difference in how solo people and group members rated the experience afterward', the researchers found, according to an item on *New York* magazine's Science of Us site. 'Everyone had the same amount of fun'.

It's not a penalty to spend time alone. It's an opportunity – to exist totally free of anyone else's expectations, or your smartphone.

EXHAUST A PLACE

French writer Georges Perec, best known for his 1978 novel *Life, A User's Manual,* coined the term *infra-ordinary* to describe the opposite of the 'extraordinary' events and objects and communications that dominate our mental lives.

Perec's obsession with the infra-ordinary was in part ideological – it critiqued the media of his time. 'What speaks to us, seemingly, is always the big event, the untoward, the extra-ordinary: the front-page splash, the banner headlines', he wrote in 1973. One can only imagine what Perec would make of the twenty-first-century 'news' cycle.

'The daily papers talk of everything except the daily', he complained. 'What's really going on, what we're experiencing, the rest, all the rest, where is it?' That's his deeper question: What about everything else?

Perec's boldest effort to try to pay the infra-ordinary its due attention took the form of a slender, lovely book called *An Attempt at Exhausting a Place in Paris,* published in 1975. To write it, he planted himself for the better part of three days on a particular Parisian plaza – disregarding the spectacular architecture and instead noting everything that came into his field of vision. His list – a postal van, a child with a dog, a woman with a newspaper, a man with a large A on his sweater – became poetry of the everyday.

I think about Perec's work most often in one of my least-favourite places: the airport. If I'm stuck in a long security line, I try to channel him and make a mental catalogue of the details and absurdities around me. (Instead of disregarding, say, a guy in a T-shirt that reads 'Old School', I ruminate on it.) This helps pass the time.

Taking notes would sharpen one's focus. And I wish some brilliant and diligent observer would try to match Perec, but in the setting of a modern airport. I have spent many hours waiting out flight delays in Atlanta and I cannot think of a more daring literary experiment than *An Attempt to Exhaust Hartsfield-Jackson International Airport.*

INVENT A NARRATION FOR QUOTIDIAN FOOTAGE

The short 1976 film *The Girl Chewing Gum* by John Smith portrays a not particularly interesting corner near a cinema in Hackney, London, in black and white. A trailer dominates the frame. A voice-over commands: 'Slowly move the trailer to the left, and I want the little girl to run across—now'.

The trailer moves slowly to the left; a little girl darts by. The voice keeps intoning what seem to be directions, over what sounds like authentic ambient noise: 'Right, now I want the old man with white hair and glasses to cross the road. Come on, quickly!' 'Put the cigarette in your mouth. Good'. Figures move across the screen and appear to be doing whatever this voice dictates.

It took me about thirty seconds to realise that the narration was devised and added after the footage was filmed to lend the illusion of direction and intent to what is in fact completely random activity. Eventually the voice-over edges towards the surreal, explaining where certain pedestrians are going or describing their inner thoughts. The speaker begins describing a field miles away, where he claims he is actually standing; finally he falls silent and the film cuts to footage of a field.

The Girl Chewing Gum is terrific and has been recognised for its subversive critique of the artifice that attaches to film as a medium. You can even find tributes on YouTube, where other people add postscripted narration to quotidian footage.

The film is also an impressive display of considered observation. Smith has studied this footage and carefully dissected minute details of movement and action and behaviour in order to retroactively construct those 'instructions'. This may be clearest (spoiler alert!) when he calls for 'the

> How should we take account of, question,
>
> describe what happens every day and recurs
>
> every day: the banal, the quotidian, the obvious,
>
> the common, the ordinary, the infra-ordinary,
>
> the background noise, the habitual?
>
> GEORGES PEREC

girl with the chewing gum' to make her appearance. A young woman promptly strides by, looking for all the world like someone who has been coached to chomp as visibly as possible as she glances in the direction of the camera. She seems so theatrical that it's hard not to laugh out loud.

Imagine if Georges Perec had a video camera instead of a notebook and recorded the daily activity on that Parisian square. The impulse is similar, but Smith selectively imposes his poetry, largely by way of a degree of paying careful attention that strikes me as a genuine feat.

You can simply use your smartphone to capture a few minutes of activity in a public space. Scrutinise it and compose a narrative that directs the figures and the camera's movements; notice how details you missed in real time start to emerge with repeated viewings.

NAME THAT THING

'I see many more Hollow Ways now that I know what one is', says Nicola Twilley, the writer and cohost of the *Gastropod* podcast. 'And I spot crown shyness now that I know it as a named phenomenon'.

I had to look up these terms. A *holloway* is a stretch of road sunk significantly below the land it passes through. *Crown shyness* describes how fully developed trees of certain species avoid touching one another, leaving distinct gaps in the arboreal canopy.

This makes Twilley's point: knowing what a thing is called makes that thing suddenly more visible. 'More than an identity, a creature's name is also a password', science and nature writer Ferris Jabr once observed; it's hard to research or otherwise learn much about the small brown bird you just noticed – but you can find out quite a lot once you know it's a house sparrow.

Start by being alert to unfamiliar vocabulary dropped by expert acquaintances: I have specific memories of learning the terms *bollard*, *plinth* and *desire path* this way (and, subsequently, noticing each all over the place). Don't let those words slide because they don't mean anything to you; latch on to them and learn what you can.

You can also ask simple questions of friends or colleagues. If you're hanging out with a nature buff, make it a point to specifically inquire about, for instance, some bit of fauna – anything from a flower to a weed, just whatever catches your eye. Get an architect to clue you in to the name of some feature of a house or building. People enjoy sharing this sort of knowledge. The more interested you seem, the more arcane they'll get. Goad them.

Alternately, try the opposite. Go online or buy a book of, for example, architectural terms and set about spotting them in the real world – maybe pick one a week. Finally, keep an eye out for stuff that *probably* has a name, but you have no idea what it might be. Make it a personal challenge to find out.

MAKE AN INVENTORY

For a 2015 BOOK called *Everything We Touch*, London-based designer and researcher Paula Zuccotti asked subjects – of various ages and professions, in a variety of countries – to document every object they touched during a twenty-four-hour period. She subsequently photographed each individual's object array. 'The items tell surprisingly intimate tales of the people who picked them up', The *Guardian* later wrote.

At its heart, *Everything We Touch* is a series of inventories. And making an inventory – any inventory – is an easy way to focus attention on things you habitually ignore.

Say you're stuck in a waiting room, bored out of your mind. Instead of seething or resorting to Facebook, make an inventory. Notice each object around you and decide why it's there.

This simple procedure is actually the starting point for many creative undertakings, large and small. The artist and educator Kate Bingaman-Burt has her students list and then draw personal inventories: everything they are carrying or everything they own that they want to get rid of.

Use these inventory prompts, then invent your own. An inventory can reveal something about a space. It can also reveal something about you.

MAKE AN INVENTORY OF THINGS YOU DIDN'T BUY

Imagine a museum of everything you thought about obtaining but didn't. What would it say about you? What can you learn from all that you desired, however fleetingly, and yet never possessed?

Designer and entrepreneur Tina Roth Eisenberg, who runs the popular blog *swissmiss*, once shared with her followers a picture of a list she'd made of 'Things I Didn't Buy'. It included expensive items like an Amazon Echo and more day-to-day consumables like Fancy Latte, which, according to the tally on her list, she had *not* bought on thirteen different occasions.

Eisenberg cited the influence of tidying guru Marie Kondo – suggesting, in effect, a kind of preemptive version of decluttering. There's something appealing about what I suppose we can call pre-decluttering: taking the idea of discarding stuff into the realm of the never owned and making that curiously concrete.

Eisenberg hit upon interesting territory to explore. 'Between stimulus and response there is a space', Viktor Frankl, the Austrian psychiatrist and neurologist wrote. 'In that space is our power to choose our response'.

What is there in this space? What fills the realm of that which we wanted, but only for a time, and that we never really did come to possess?

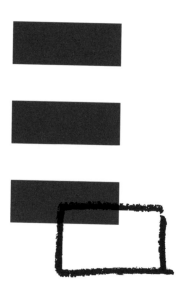

MAKE AN IMMATERIAL INVENTORY

At a relatively early stage of his career, the artist and illustrator Brian Rea found himself making lists of things he was worried about. He started asking others what *they* were worried about. And then he was invited to create a mural as part of a group show in Barcelona.

He came up with 'a huge, handwritten mural of fears', as the designer and writer Debbie Millman later described it, based on the 'inventory of things [he] and other people were worried about'.

In a way, Rea reflected later, this 9 metres-wide, 4.5 metres-tall piece – which functioned like a monumental infographic – was a snapshot of the political climate at the time and a means of understanding how his own worries connected to others.

Since then, Rea has continued to keep unusual lists: memorable moments during a dinner party, the celebrities he's spotted in Los Angeles, the bars he visited when he lived in Stockholm. Such lists amount to idiosyncratic, immaterial inventories.

They're informal and original time capsules.

Make your own.

MAKE AN INSANELY DETAILED INVENTORY

👁 👁 👁 👁

I've long held a fascination with the so-called quantified-self movement. Also a dose of scepticism about it.

The idea of the quantified self generally involves using technologies to track and 'quantify' one's existence (from how one moves to what one eats to all the minuscule actions that make up a day) and to analyse the resulting data, presumably with an eye towards self-improvement.

Perhaps this seems like a bloodless and/or dopey way to live. And perhaps it is.

Yet I remain intrigued by those who find it productive or satisfying, and I follow occasional quantified-self news. Which is how I learned of someone called Matt Manhattan.

Manhattan is a quantified-self enthusiast. According to quantified self.com, he 'takes inventory of every item he owns: shirts, ice cream containers, paper towels, you name it'. To what end? Well, it's a practise that 'changed the way he thought about his possessions, and, as a side effect, ended up saving him a substantial amount of money'. He claims to have become a more thoughtful and considered consumer, because he is able to capture and 'reflect on' these raw details that other people don't notice.

His process involved an Excel spreadsheet that listed every article of clothing he owns, as well as its price, date of acquisition, brand, colour, and similar data. This allowed him to generate a variety of charts and graphs from which he could see, at a glance, that he owned eleven T-shirts, purchased for an average price of $21.95 each. A pie chart revealed his wardrobe was less colourful than he had assumed. Incredibly, he *photographed* every article of clothing in his possession – rather nicely, on a uniform white background – and built an enormous wardrobe-overview blog post.

As a practical exercise, this is ridiculous. But as a *ridiculous* exercise, it's sublime.

So go ahead. Pick some category – clothing, kitchenware, everything in your bedroom, anything at all – and create a detailed inventory.

Record your insights. Determine whether these insights suggest changes you should make to your behaviour. Monitor whether you make these changes or ignore the data.

Make an inventory of:

THINGS YOU TOUCH

SOUNDS

THINGS YOU DIDN'T BUY

YOUR WORRIES

MEMORABLE MOMENTS

ALL OF YOUR POSSESSIONS

ASK: HOW DID IT GET THAT WAY?

The writer Paul Lukas loves to spot interesting details in the designed world that the rest of us missed and he has a remarkable skill for this practise that he's called 'inconspicuous consumption'. It's useful, he suggested to me, to question what's right in front of us. Don't overthink this, just ask a basic question: How did that get that way?

'We often take for granted that the physical world, and especially the built environment, just sort of happened out of nowhere', he says. But actually, everything has a back story – from a skyscraper all the way down to the door handles in the offices of that skyscraper.

I suspect we take many human-made things *even more* for granted than we do the natural. Think about, say, the stop sign. Stop signs are as familiar as clouds. When you look at the clouds, you probably know, or at least

> We take for granted that certain things are a certain way because we're used to seeing them that way . . . Once you start asking what the back stories are, you start noticing more and more things, each with its own story.
>
> PAUL LUKAS

have a hunch, that there is some kind of scientific explanation behind their shapes, density or precise white-to-dark colouration. You may not know or even care exactly how each one got that way – but you know it's a function of something and you know that you *could* know the details.

Weirdly, the octagonal shape of a stop sign seems much more like something that *just is*; we are more likely to wonder or at least speculate about the shape of the cloud.

But of course stop signs have a back story. Did you know that road signs are designed to signal the level of danger drivers need to be aware of by the number of sides they have? And stop signs, having eight sides, signal the second highest? (The round and thus effectively infinite-sided sign used to mark railway crossings is the highest level.)

Identify one thing that you've taken for granted your entire life and ask how it got that way. **Find out the back story.** And do the same thing again tomorrow.

READ THE LABEL

The labels we find in, say, the inside of the neck of a mass-produced T-shirt tell stories. A basic disclosure of material composition (the percentage that is cotton, for example), a declaration that the thing was 'Made in Wherever'. We hardly notice these particulars.

The Canadian Fair Trade Network, in an effort to underscore why we should be paying more attention to the wheres and hows of our manufactured purchases, once ran a provocative ad campaign that played off the innocuous nature of the clothing label. In a series of images, it presented garments with detailed tags – some of them more than 30cm long and jammed with text. For instance:

100% cotton. Made in Cambodia by Behnly, nine years old. He gets up at 5:00 am every morning to make his way to the garment factory where he works. It will be dark when he arrives and dark when

he leaves. He dresses lightly because the temperature in the room he works reaches 30 degrees. The dust in the room fills his nose and mouth. He will make less than a dollar, for a day spent slowly suffo-cating. A mask would cost the company ten cents. The label doesn't tell the whole story.

Presumably Behnly's story is actually an amalgam based on a knowledge of typical work conditions. But it's jarring. And it makes you appreciate the clothing tag in a different way.

Of course we can't really know the story of a garment and of course not everything made in Cambodia (or wherever) is a product of human suffering. But next time you're browsing the clothes rack or your own wardrobe, read the tags.

Scrutinise whatever information is available.

Consider what information is *not* available. Imagine why that might be – and what you may be missing.

MAKE A PERSONAL MAP

The organizers of a project called 'Where You Are' asked sixteen writers and artists to make maps – but of a very particular kind.

Photographer and writer Valeria Luiselli's 'Swings of Harlem' documented a specific piece of playground equipment across a particular geographic area.

Denis Wood, known in part for his original thinking on cartography, hand-drew a map as memoir (titled 'The Paper Route Empire') to capture Cleveland as it exists in his childhood memories.

Novelist Adam Thirlwell mapped 'Places I've Nearly Been to but Have Not'. Author and artist Leanne Shapton painted 'tablescapes', depicting objects on her desk at various moments.

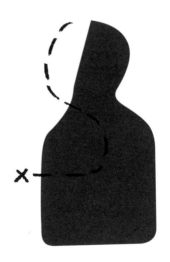

These projects were fascinating because they portrayed the artists' *personal* maps. Devising these documents required creative and careful observation.

Think, then, about the variety of territories you may know or seek to know. Using paper and pen, your smartphone camera or whatever medium you like, make your own personal map.

- Map the points of interest within your home, according to your dog.

- Map the most boring features of your commute.

- Map the sounds of your neighbourhood.

- Map the textures in your office.

- Map your favourite flavours around town.

- Map the empty shelf slots of out-of-stock products at your local supermarket.

Keep going.

KEEP A WEEKLY LIST

'Experts in authoritarianism advise to keep a list of things subtly changing around you, so you'll remember'. So reads the recurring headline on the Medium.com account of Amy Siskind, a left-leaning activist alarmed by the political climate. She created a dedicated site called theweeklylist.org to document 'ways in which she saw America's taken-for-granted governmental norms changing', *Washington Post* media columnist Margaret Sullivan wrote.

You may be sympathetic to Siskind's political point of view or you may be hostile to it. Set that aside for a moment. Because making a weekly list of 'things subtly changing around you' takes some observational dedication. It could be a method of tracking a neighbourhood, a town, a relationship or your own life.

Faythe Levine, an artist and documentary filmmaker in Wisconsin, recommends 'ongoing lists' of whatever people, places and things are interesting you at any given time. 'Revisit them every so often when you need inspiration or fodder', she advises.

Less than a year into her process, Siskind told an interviewer it was instructive (well, she used the word *scary*) to 'see what we've already gotten used to'.

Most change is gradual, but surely *something* changed in your neighbourhood, your office, your romantic life this week. What was it?

Take note. Revisit your findings. Note the trends. Note what you'd forgotten. Note what you've accepted as normal.

ENJOY A HANGOVER

Drinking too much is a bad idea and I'm not here to endorse it.

Some of you, however, will do it anyway, perhaps in part to experience the curious effects that alcohol can have on perception – heightening some feelings while suppressing others. That's really none of my business. But I will pass along one piece of surprising advice from my friend Josh Glenn: when the morning after rolls around, don't try to squelch your hangover. Because it's not a problem, he argues. It's an opportunity.

'So what's good about a hangover?' Glenn has written. 'The hungover person is abnormally aware of sights, sounds (everything seems TOO LOUD!), tastes, odours, and textures which normally would go unremarked. That's a good thing, not a bad thing. The hungover eye, for instance, because it is neither obstructed by the blinders of our everyday biases, nor deceived by intoxicated hallucinations, is magnetically attracted to seemingly ordinary objects which take on an incredible, luminous significance: anyone who has ever experienced the "stares" when hung over knows exactly what I mean'.

Glenn compares the hung-over state to conditions of nirvana or grace.

You may or may not take his thinking seriously here – and I certainly don't recommend a drunken binge for the sole purpose of obtaining a hangover. But should you find yourself in an altered state, you ought to inhabit it fully rather than struggle to find a shortcut out. Embrace it instead 'as a form of reaggregation from the extraordinary into the ordinary, as a "middle state" of perception in which one can for a brief time see the usual in an unusual manner'.

And if you conclude that this unusual manner isn't one you enjoy, perhaps you'll remember that the next time you start drinking.

> When you wake up in the morning, I think you do not feel so well. Your mind is full of 'weeds' . . . But if you can cease striving to overcome those weeds, they, too, can enrich your path to enlightenment.
>
> SHUNRYU SUZUKI

TAKE A MINDFUL SHOWER

Writer Libby Copeland used to find the shower 'terrifying'. Why? Because there she had to be alone with her thoughts and she wanted distraction. So she tried 'mindful showering'. Don't laugh. Copeland describes an easy introduction to attending to immediate experience: '**I try to notice one thing each time**, whether it's the goose bumps that rise when the hot water first hits, or the false urgency of the thoughts that still come', she wrote in *The Smithsonian* magazine. 'They demand I follow them, but they're almost always riddles that can't be solved'.

Suddenly a routine shower seems potentially poetic. Mindfulness and meditation practises that involve long minutes just sitting and thinking about breathing can be intimidating. The shower, on the other hand, is standard fare.

Try to focus on one thing next time you're in the privacy of a shower.

STUDY A ROCK

Mindfulness can be a confusing concept – the term seems vague enough to be defined however you wish. But it needn't be intimidating. A child could do it.

In fact, *The New York Times* published a lengthy interactive package on the subject of 'Mindfulness for Children', which defined mindfulness as 'a simple technique that emphasises paying attention to the present moment in an accepting, nonjudgmental manner'.

One exercise, an audio guide narrated by mindfulness instructor and author Annaka Harris, lasts five minutes and involves a small stone or rock. 'We'll pay attention to what it's like to look very closely at something, noticing all the details we see right now, in this moment', Harris soothingly begins.

(Maybe this sounds ridiculous. But set aside any I'm-not-a-child objections and at least consider the spirit here.)

Sit on the floor with your legs crossed, Harris continues, and place your 'focus rock' in front of you. Rest your hands on your knees, sitting up straight but staying relaxed. Feel your feet and legs resting on the floor and your hands touching your legs. Close your eyes and focus on your breathing for half a minute or so.

'This moment has never happened before', Harris says. Each breath is different from the last. Every moment is new. Take another few seconds to reflect on that and to breathe.

Now open your eyes and consider your focus rock. 'What does it look like?' Harris asks. 'Do you see spots or lines?' Notice the shape, the outline, the colour (or colours). Look very closely. Notice new things. What you notice might even change as you look. Look for at least a minute. Relax your body. Remain silent. Look for another thirty seconds.

'You've probably never looked this closely at a rock before, right?' Harris concludes. Breath and stretch. Try it again sometime, with a leaf or a shell or another rock or even this same one.

Anything becomes interesting

if you look at it long enough.

GUSTAVE FLAUBERT

EMPATHISE WITH A ROCK

According to Maria Popova, the concept of empathy 'originated in the contemplation of art'. She cites Mark Rothko, for instance, declaring that someone who is moved by one of his paintings is experiencing some version of Rothko's own emotions when he was creating it.

But as art and science cross-pollinated, she writes, empathy was 'imported . . . into popular culture', largely by psychology. Popova, in an essay on her site BrainPickings.org, points in particular to the insights of philosopher Theodor Lipps, who had a special interest in the impact of art. 'Central to Lipps's invention of empathy was his notion of *einsehen,* or "inseeing"', she continues, which is 'a kind of conscious observation'. To define the term more specifically, she cites author Rachel Corbett, who in *You Must Change Your Life* offers this:

> *If faced with a rock, for instance, one should stare deep into the place where its rockness begins to form. Then the observer should keep looking until his own centre starts to sink with the stony weight of the rock forming inside him, too. It is a kind of perception that takes place within the body, and it requires the observer to be both the seer and the seen. To observe with empathy, one sees not only with the eyes but with the skin.*

In other words, it is one thing to catalogue or internally describe and memorise the attributes of a rock. Empathising with a rock – or an artwork or any other object – is something else entirely.

Do this.

INTERVIEW AN OBJECT

In connection with one of her exhibitions at the Museum of Modern Art, curator Paola Antonelli interviewed a number of people on the subject of material culture. One of her questions stood out: 'What object', she wanted to know, 'would you take to lunch?'

One way to perceive an object is to consider the questions it raises – even if they are questions it can't literally answer, insofar as it remains an object. But if you *could* interrogate your computer about how and where it was assembled or have a discussion with your grandmother's necklace that you inherited about the world it witnessed or ask a found coin how it ended up on the pavement – wouldn't you?

Think of an object that raises questions that only the object itself could answer. Thinking about the questions you would ask of that object clarifies what you see and what it means – to you.

It took me a while to figure out what object I'd most like to interrogate. But I settled on the atomic bomb.

I have so many questions. How would such an object think about itself?

EMBRACE DISTRACTION

In his charming book *Wasting Time on the Internet,* Kenneth Goldsmith offers a cheery defence of our distraction-filled lives. André Breton, he notes, proposed 'sleepwalking as an optimal widespread social condition'. Thus the pedestrians lost in the phones, oblivious to their surroundings, socialising with distant others, are, like sleepwalkers, 'both present and absent' – and isn't the 'twilight between wakefulness and sleep' rather comparable to the 'surrealists' ideal state for making art'?

Enabled by our connected devices, we are 'awash in a new electronic collective unconscious', Goldsmith writes. 'I can't help notice we've become very good at being distracted. Breton would be delighted'.

In short, to be distracted is to concentrate, however fleetingly, on something besides whatever you intended to concentrate on – and accepting that this distraction is a *form* of concentration.

The implication is that if we focus with perfect discipline, we actually miss out on 'the surprises that distraction can bring', Goldsmith

Pay attention.

Be astonished.

Tell about it.

MARY OLIVER

writes. 'True, distraction might mean missing the main event. But what if nobody knows what or where the main event is?'

The book ends with a long list of suggestions for wasting time on the internet – or, really, with technology. These are much more active and subversive than just going with the digital flow. A lot of Goldsmith's ideas are in fact extremely labour-intensive. For instance, 'Using Google Maps satellite view, stitch together a new city. Give it a name, and invent laws for it'.

But here's one that captures what it can mean to embrace a distraction and give it considered attention:

'In a public place', Goldsmith suggests, 'record the noise you hear with your phone. Then go to a silent private place and listen to it. **Send the noise to a partner and ask them where they think it is from**'.

TREASURE THE DREGS

'Dregs are the sweetest drink', Rick Prelinger once wrote. For proof, look no further than *No More Road Trips?*, one of several feature-length films he has created, entirely by weaving together passages from old, discarded home movies. By collecting and mining these 'dregs', he created a remarkable meditation on the heyday of the American road trip, stretching through the middle decades of the twentieth century.

I saw *No More Road Trips?* at the Full Frame Documentary Film Festival in Durham, North Carolina, a few years ago and I was struck by Prelinger's advice to audience members making home movies today. 'Please', he said, 'film the gas stations'.

Later, I asked him to say more about this. 'When people pick up a home movie camera and look through it, typically they film something or someone that they love', he said. Thus the bulk of any given home movie is meant to be picturesque – pretty flowers, mountain ranges, blue skies, and other aesthetic pleasures that might resemble our Instagram feeds now.

What's much more valuable, he continued, are the home movies that 'feature the everyday'. One of his favourites came from a travelling Coca-Cola salesman who, for reasons we'll never know, filmed 'the most depressed, hardscrabble general stores' in his southern Ohio territory in the early 1930s.

Petrol stations are an example of 'what's hardest to remember', Prelinger concluded. 'We can remember Disneyland, and we can remember what the Grand Canyon looked like'. But how interesting is that to look at again? 'I guarantee you that if you were to shoot those lottery ticket dealers and the fireworks stands and the gas stations where they

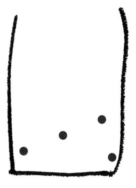

now have a TV in the gas pump or the convenience stores that have the bulletproof partitions between you and the clerks – that's the thing to remember about today's road trip', he said. 'These are the things that over time will change and are very much tied to our historical era. And that's what we should shoot'.

It's a compelling challenge: what *are* the everyday details of our time that might seem most telling and compelling to future generations? They're hard to spot and might seem crazy to document. **But even the attempt to identify the quintessentially uninteresting can be revelatory.**

And it's an example of what Prelinger meant when he encouraged people to celebrate the dregs in a manifesto he wrote a while back, 'On the Virtues of Preexisting Material'.

Back in the 1980s and 1990s, Prelinger amassed a collection of old industrial and educational films. These were mostly neglected or discarded at the time, but he tracked them down and acquired them with ferocious determination. Over time he convinced others to see the import of this trove – which was eventually acquired by the Library of Congress.

'I was struck by how much of the history of working people was contained in films made by corporations', he wrote in his manifesto. 'In order to extract it you've got to engage in selective appropriation, but it's there, often eloquently so'. He pointed to a 1936 film intended to glorify mass production at Chevrolet.

'[W]hat it really shows is how elemental, dangerous and mind-numbing the work at Flint was', he wrote. 'It's a film no one else seems to have, and it's now on the National Film Registry, but it was dregs – on a cold day in 1983, I paid a man not to throw it away'.

TRACK THE MOON

In his book *Present Shock: When Everything Happens Now,* the technology and culture critic Douglas Rushkoff lamented the disconnected lives many of us have come to live and encouraged his readers to connect with the natural world.

Asked by an interviewer for tips on combating 'present shock', he started with this: 'Try to stay aware of what time of day it is and what cycle of the moon that you're in . . . try to look at the night sky each night'.

I suspect that for much of the existence of the species, the human animal was keenly aware of the moon, the night sky's most prominent feature and a marker of cyclical time.

Do *you* know what phase the moon is in right now?

DO IT AGAIN

Artist Adam Henry uses repetition in his work 'to set up parameters of comparison and to slow down the viewing experience'. This reflects his own cultural consumption habits. Rereading a particular book or watching the same movie over and over is 'a way for me to understand and study the logic behind things', he told the online art magazine *Hyperallergic*. 'For the last three years I have read and reread the same book on every trip I've taken. I think I'm up to nine reads. It's been an incredible experience to try to truly know this book and how the content changes depending on the place where I am reading it'. The book, incidentally, is *The Invention of Morel* by the Argentinean writer Adolfo Bioy Casares.

I suspect we all share mixed feelings about repetitious cultural consumption. There is so much to take in, there is so much else to do and enjoy – not just the new, but the classic we haven't made time for yet. This makes the act of returning to a known favourite feel like some variety of squalor.

Resist that feeling. Pick some cultural object right now that made an impression on you and make it a top priority to revisit it.

Maybe this experience will be disappointing or maybe it will be invigorating. Doesn't matter. Take it for what it is.

Consider how you have changed and how you haven't. Consider whether you should return to the same cultural object one year from now.

Try to make the answer affirmative and try to follow through.

CONNOISSEUR SOMETHING AWFUL

With a high nasal voice, a charismatic giggle and an infectious enthusiasm for cities in all their splendid detail, Timothy 'Speed' Levitch is the most memorable tour guide you will encounter. He's been at it, off and on, since the early 1990s, in San Francisco, Kansas City, New York and elsewhere. His remarkable narrations concerning New York City for the patrons of official tour buses – ecstatic soliloquies and dazzling rants on the glory of terracotta or the unspeakable shame of the grid street pattern – formed the basis of a wildly entertaining 1998 documentary called *The Cruise*.

What Levitch calls *cruising* can be thought of as one of two modes of moving through the world. The other mode, and the far more common one, is what he calls *commuter consciousness*. 'The commute begins, I believe, in that moment when our urge to get to our destination becomes even more alive than our selves', he once explained. **'COMMUTING, active verb, is to travel along with the assumption that every godforsaken human being currently on this planet is in my way'**.

He paused to giggle after he said this and then described an alternative to the commuter mind-set. **'CRUISING, also a verb, active verb, is the immediate appreciation of the beauty immediately around you in your immediacy'**, he continued; it's 'a natural antidepressive'.

Levitch has offered what he calls the Rush Hour Tour. Participants meet at five p.m. by the information desk in the middle of New York's Grand Central Terminal – exactly when absolutely no one wants to be there. Levitch cackles. 'Yeah . . . It's a tour of what everyone is trying to get away from'.

To get his tour groups into the proper frame of mind, he informs participants that the group will inhabit the mind-set of a Greek chorus, deconstructing the action unfolding before them; riffing, as in a performed drama, on the potential meanings behind the behaviours occupying the stage that is our world. 'A *private* Greek chorus', he clarifies, 'observing, commenting, participating – but not really committing'. *In* the scene, but not *of* the scene. 'Eventually', he says, 'you're viewing rush hour as a parody dance of our interconnectedness'.

As an example of what that means, Levitch advises, delightfully: 'Connoisseur that honk'.

This shtick (as he frankly characterised it to me) is something he uses as the group moves out of Grand Central and into the overtrafficked streets of Midtown, plangent with motors and horns. 'As each of the different honks of the city comes tumbling into your present tense', he instructs, 'take a moment to taste and connoisseur that honk – based on its voluminousness, its intensity, context and duration. Taste and connoisseur'.

Sometimes he'll say all this right after a notably obnoxious honk, which he will proceed to describe in disconcerting detail: how its pitch compares to other honks, what its duration suggests about the honker's goals, what sort of vehicle such a honk implies and so on. But almost as often he'll have just finished sketching the general idea of urban honking when a particularly earsplitting example will cut him off. 'The city', he says, 'is a genius vaudeville partner'.

You can 'connoisseur' anything – and the more unappealing the subject, the better. Levitch concedes that some of his customers do not appreciate this riff, because it makes them notice, with fresh intensity, something that they'd trained themselves to tune out. But that's precisely the charm of the practise: to convert a signal annoyance of humdrum life into a thing that might be savoured.

The real trick of the *cruise* is accepting that we are able to practise it in our most mundane moments – to cruise through a mindless job or a tedious task or an annoying scenario. It's a coping strategy: Levitch's family moved to the suburbs when he was a child and he grew up with an acute sense of feeling isolated. 'I think that maybe that was my initial innate need to appreciate the beauty immediately', he said. 'Because if I didn't make the suburbs interesting, I was *done*. It was almost like an action thriller movie – but curiosity is the hero'.

Levitch observes that as a tour guide he often encounters people who seem to be making 'desperate attempts to be on vacation'. They're working at leisure like some fearsome job, radiating the misery of failed expectation. 'I'm working a nine-hour shift', he says, 'and I'm definitely more on vacation than they are'. He has elsewhere raised this idea. **The *lebenskünstler* – one of those untranslatable German words that, by one definition, 'connotes a person who approaches life with the zest and inspiration of an artist, although he or she may not be working recognisably as an artist'.**

An interviewer once asked Levitch if the *cruise* was essentially a Buddhist notion. He replied: 'Perhaps appreciating the beauty of the outside world is eventually appreciating the beauty inside', I believe this is true.

MAKE AN APPOINTMENT . . . WITH YOURSELF

A few years ago, comedian and filmmaker Mike Birbiglia realised that as rigorously as he scheduled his time to deal with projects and commitments, he was neglecting something. 'I was showing up to, like, lunch meetings or business meetings, but I wasn't showing up to meet myself', he told an interviewer. 'And so I wrote a note next to my bed – this is so corny – but I wrote: "Mike, exclamation point, you have an appointment at Café Pedlar at seven a.m. . . . with your mind"'.

There's something powerful about blocking out time in this way. Birbiglia's approach reminds me of a suggestion from author Julia Cameron, one that's at the heart of her very popular book *The Artist's Way*. Cameron instructs her students – her programme is built around the idea of 'recovering' creativity – to schedule weekly 'artist dates'. As she has described it, this means 'a once-weekly, festive, solo expedition to explore something that interests you'. No significant other; no looking after your niece. Something for you.

For Cameron, this is for the artist or aspiring artist within you – but does not necessarily involve a formal trip to a museum. **'What you are trying to do is sort of enchant yourself'**, she has said.

It is, after all, a date. One friend of mine, Diana Kimball Berlin, worked her way through the whole *Artist's Way* programme and blogged about the experience. So by way of example, her artist dates included shopping at art supply stores, attending a cello performance, visiting a 'Balinese-themed' spa, and going to 'a smoothie shop in a shipping container, followed by a documentary'.

Oddly, Cameron has found people tend to resist this instruction to devote such time to themselves. 'We understand the work ethic', she muses, 'so we will go *work* on our creativity. But we won't necessarily go *play* on our creativity. And yet **playing is absolutely necessary**'.

Cameron is not the only one who believes in the value of such personal time. The life-hack-focused *New York Times* Smarter Living newsletter has advised: 'Take time to reflect. Schedule it in your calendar and give yourself the space to think. You'll make progress even if it's just a few hours every other week'.

And a group of academic researchers, specifically looking at how to make the most of, or at least cope with, commuting time, posited the notion of a 'pocket of freedom'. This turned on a focus on what individuals can control – in this case, how to spend one's time. Maybe the most notable thing about their project, as they described it in the *Harvard Business Review,* is the fact that the phrase *pocket of freedom* was borrowed from one researcher's great-aunt, who spent her early adulthood in the ghettos of Nazi-occupied Poland.

'No matter how hungry, tired or frightened she was', the researchers wrote, 'she devoted one hour each night to a creative activity with her niece – a practise that, she later noted, helped her persevere'. Surely if someone living under such circumstances can carve out an hour, so can I and so can you.

All those notions are distinct, yet fundamentally similar:

- Scheduling creative play
- Scheduling personal reflection
- Scheduling specific passion-project focus

What unites them is a commitment to making the time to attend to what really matters to you – a sort of jujitsu on the culture of scheduling and commitment that hogs so much of our attention.

When Birbiglia met with himself, he worked on a screenplay that he'd been thinking about a lot. But you don't need to spend your time with yourself working on anything. Maybe you just need to show up at Café Pedlar (or wherever) and commit to absolutely no distractions from whatever you want to think about.

Experience the place you're in. Mull a personal matter or some combination of them. Or perhaps commit yourself to executing one of the other exercises in this book.

It's so easy to build our time around and commit to obligations from without. Maybe it's not so hard to hijack that instinct and use it to trick ourselves into committing to ourselves.

CARE FOR SOMETHING

I'll close with an idea from a former student named Miguel Olivares, who presented his solution to my charge that he 'practise paying attention' with a near apology – worrying aloud that he'd misunderstood the assignment. He had made a planter, he explained, for a cactus. He'd done this, he said, on the theory that 'by nurturing or caring for something, you pay more attention to it'.

While this wasn't exactly what I had in mind, he had nailed the assignment. For starters, there are countless ways to define 'paying attention', and even this book-length list is woefully incomplete.

But really, *caring* is at the very heart of it all.

These exercises and meditations were designed expressly to help you decide what *you* want to care about – and thus what and whom you want to care for and attend to.

This at its core is the art and the joy of noticing.

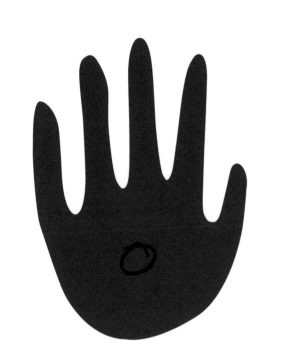

Our life experience will equal what we have

paid attention to, whether by choice or default.

WILLIAM JAMES

An Epilogue

INVENT AN EXERCISE IN NOTICING

One last thing.

Maybe you, in the course of exploring this book, had ideas of your own for fun or provocative things you can do to help you notice or pay attention in a more useful and joyful manner. Even if you haven't thought of something specific, it wouldn't surprise me if you had some gestating idea or two, so I want to encourage you to pursue that. Go back through the book if you need to and invent your own exercise.

Give it a try.

Tell a friend about it. Or share it as you wish. Or tell me – visit **robwalker.net/noticing** and get in touch, or subscribe there to The Art of Noticing newsletter.

I'd love to hear what you come up with – and what you noticed.

ACKNOWLEDGEMENTS

I owe much, to many. What can I say? Only this.

Thank you, Allan Chochinov, the staff, the faculty and most of all the students of the School of Visual Arts Products of Design programme.

Thank you, Vera Titunik. Thank you, Josh Glenn. Thank you, Cynthia Joyce. Thank you, Austin Kleon. Thank you, Kate Bingaman-Burt.

Thank you, Kenneth Goldsmith. Thank you, Paul Lukas, Marc Weidenbaum, Paola Antonelli, Nick Gray, Alex Kalman, Nina Katchadourian, Davy Rothbart, Charlie Todd, Speed Levitch, Rita J. King, Dan Ariely, Rick Prelinger, Ingrid Fetell Lee, Seth Godin, Sarah Rich, Lucian James, Rotten Apple, Carla Diana, Geoff Manaugh, Nicola Twilley, Ethan Hein, Faythe Levine, Tom Weis, Jim Coudal, Matthew Fry Jacobson, Matt Green, William Helmreich, Debbie Millman, Charles Duhigg and Beth Mosher.

Thank you, Alice Twemlow, Molly Heintz and the staff and participants in the SVA D*Crit/Design Research summer intensive programme.

Thank you, Steven Heller. Thank you, Andrew Leland. Thank you, Alex Balk. Thank you, Stacy Switzer. Thank you, G. K. Darby. Thank you, David Dunton. Thank you, David Shields.

Thank you thank you thank you, Matt McGowan.

Thank you, Oliver Munday and Peter Mendelsund! Thank you, Sonny Mehta, Chris Gillespie, Kelly Blair, Maggie Hinders, Rita Madrigal, Nancy Inglis, Lisa Silverman, Paul Bogaards, Erinn Hartman, Rachel Fershleiser, Emily Murphy, Lorie Young and the whole team at Alfred A. Knopf. Maria Goldverg: I cannot possibly thank you enough.

Thank you, M&D: I love you.

And thank you, again and again, and always and for everything, to E.

SOURCES AND FURTHER READING

Inspiration for the suggestions in *The Art of Noticing* came from many sources, conversations and interviews, as noted throughout the text itself. Here are more specific citations, additional sources that I drew on and suggestions for further reading. For more details, visit robwalker.net/noticing.

Anderson, Sam. 'Letter of Recommendation: Looking Out the Window'. *The New York Times Magazine,* 9 April, 2016.

Ariely, Dan. *Predictably Irrational: The Hidden Forces That Shape Our Decisions.* New York: Harper Perennial, 2009.

Berger, John. *Ways of Seeing.* London: Penguin, 1972.

Bogost, Ian. *Play Anything: The Pleasures of Limits, the Uses of Boredom, and the Secret of Games.* New York: Basic Books, 2016.

Brunner, Bernd. 'The Art of Noises: On the Logic of Sound and the Senses'. *The Smart Set,* 1 September, 2015. https://thesmartset.com/the-art-of-noises/.

Burrington, Ingrid. *Networks of New York: An Illustrated Field Guide to Urban Internet Infrastructure.* Brooklyn, NY: Melville House Publishing, 2016.

Calle, Sophie. *Suite Vénitienne.* Catskill, NY: Siglo, 2015.

Cameron, Julia. *The Artist's Way: A Spiritual Path to Higher Creativity,* 25th anniversary ed. New York: Tarcher Perigee, 2016.

Carr, Nicholas. *The Glass Cage: Automation and Us.* New York: W. W. Norton & Company, 2014.

Carroll, Lewis. *Eight or Nine Wise Words About Letter-Writing.* https://www.gutenberg.org/files/38065/38065-h/38065-h.htm.

Clébert, Jean-Paul. *Paris Vagabond,* trans. Donald Nicholson-Smith. New York: New York Review Books, 2016.

Dawson, Peter. *The Field Guide to Typography: Typefaces in the Urban Landscape.* New York: Prestel Publishing, 2013.

Forbes, Rob. *See for Yourself: A Visual Guide to Everyday Beauty.* San Francisco: Chronicle Books, 2015.

Garrett, Bradley L. *Explore Everything: Place-Hacking the City.* New York: Verso, 2013.

Glenn, Joshua and Carol Hayes. *Taking Things Seriously: 75 Objects with Unexpected Significance.* New York: Princeton Architectural Press, 2007.

Goldsmith, Kenneth. *Uncreative Writing: Managing Language in the Digital Age.* New York: Columbia University Press, 2011.

Goldsmith, Kenneth. *Wasting Time on the Internet.* New York: Harper Perennial, 2016.

Harris, Jacob. 'Why I Like to Instagram the Sky'. *The Atlantic,* 14 March, 2016. www.theatlantic.com/technology/archive/2016/03/sky-gradients/473034/.

Helmreich, William. *The New York Nobody Knows: Walking 6,000 Miles in the City.* Princeton, NJ: Princeton University Press, 2013.

Henshaw, Victoria. *Urban Smellscapes: Understanding and Designing City Smell Environments.* New York: Routledge, 2013.

Horowitz, Alexandra. *On Looking: A Walker's Guide to the Art of Observation.* New York: Scribner, 2013.

'How to Read a Landscape'. www.williamcronon.net/researching/landscapes.htm.

Huxtable, Ada Louise. *Kicked a Building Lately?* Oakland: University of California Press, 1989.

Hwang, Tim and Craig Cannon. *The Container Guide.* New York: Infrastructure Observatory Press, 2015.

Hyde, Lewis. *Trickster Makes This World: Mischief, Myth, and Art.* New York: Farrar, Straus and Giroux, 1998.

Kent, Sister Corita and Jan Steward. *Learning by Heart: Teachings to Free the Creative Spirit,* 2nd ed. New York: Allworth Press, 2008.

Kleon, Austin. *Steal Like an Artist: 10 Things Nobody Told You About Being Creative.* New York: Workman, 2012.

Krouse Rosenthal, Amy. *Textbook Amy Krouse Rosenthal.* New York: Dutton, 2016.

Langer, Ellen J. *Mindfullness: 25th Anniversary Edition.* Boston: Da Capo Press, 2014.

Manaugh, Geoff. *A Burglar's Guide to the City.* New York: Farrar, Straus and Giroux, 2016.

Montague, Julian. *The Stray Shopping Carts of Eastern North America: A Guide to Field Identification.* New York: Harry N. Abrams, 2006.

Nelson, George. *How to See: A Guide to Reading Our Man-Made Environment.* Oakland, CA: Design Within Reach, 2003.

Oliveros, Pauline. *Deep Listening: A Composer's Sound Practise.* Lincoln, NE: iUniverse, 2005.

Paper Monument, ed. *Draw It with Your Eyes Closed: The Art of the Assignment.* Brooklyn, NY: Paper Monument, 2012.

Perec, Georges. *An Attempt at Exhausting a Place in Paris,* reprint ed., trans. Marc Lowenthal. Cambridge, MA: Wakefield Press, 2010.

Pillemer, Karl. *30 Lessons for Living: Tried and True Advice from the Wisest Americans,* reprint ed. New York: Avery, 2012.

Prelinger, Rick. 'On the Virtues of Preexisting Material'. *Contents,* issue no. 5. http://contentsmagazine.com/articles/on-the-virtues-of-preexisting-material/.

Roberts, Veronica, ed. *Nina Katchadourian: Curiouser.* Austin, TX: Blanton Museum of Art, 2017.

Rushkoff, Douglas. *Present Shock: When Everything Happens Now.* New York: Current, 2013.

Russell, Jay D. 'Marcel Duchamp's Readymades: Walking on Infrathin Ice'. www.dada-companion.com/duchamp/archive/duchamp_walking_on_infrathin_ice.pdf.

Schwartz, Barry. *The Paradox of Choice: Why Less Is More,* rev. ed. New York: Ecco, 2016.

Shepard, Sam and Johnny Dark. Two Prospectors: The Letters of Sam Shepard and Johnny Dark. Austin: University of Texas Press, 2013.

Stark, Kio. *When Strangers Meet: How People You Don't Know Can Transform You.* New York: Simon & Schuster/TED, 2016.

Suzuki, Shunryu. *Zen Mind, Beginner's Mind: Informal Talks on Zen Meditation and Practise.* Boulder, CO: Shambhala, 2011.

Vanderbilt, Tom. *You May Also Like: Taste in an Age of Endless Choice.* New York: Simon & Schuster, 2016.

Wechsler, Lawrence. *Seeing Is Forgetting the Name of the Thing One Sees,* expanded ed. Berkeley and Los Angeles: University of California Press, 2008.

Wright, Robert. *Why Buddhism Is True: The Science and Philosophy of Meditation and Enlightenment.* New York: Simon & Schuster, 2017.

Wu, Tim. *The Attention Merchants: The Epic Scramble to Get Inside Our Heads.* New York: Alfred A. Knopf, 2016.

Zomorodi, Manoush. *Bored and Brilliant: How Spacing Out Can Unlock Your Most Productive and Creative Self.* New York: St. Martin's Press, 2017.

Zuccotti, Paula. *Everything We Touch: A 24-Hour Inventory of Our Lives.* New York: Viking, 2015.

A NOTE ABOUT THE AUTHOR

Rob Walker is a journalist covering design, technology, business, the arts and other subjects. He writes 'The Workologist' column for the Sunday Business section of *The New York Times* and contributes to a variety of other publications and media outlets. Previously, he was a contributing writer to *The New York Times Magazine,* where his 'Consumed' column ran from 2004 to 2011. His earlier books are *Buying In, Letters from New Orleans* and (coedited with Joshua Glenn) *Significant Objects: 100 Extraordinary Stories About Ordinary Things.* Walker is on the faculty of the Products of Design MFA-programme at the School of Visual Arts. He lives in New Orleans. www.robwalker.net